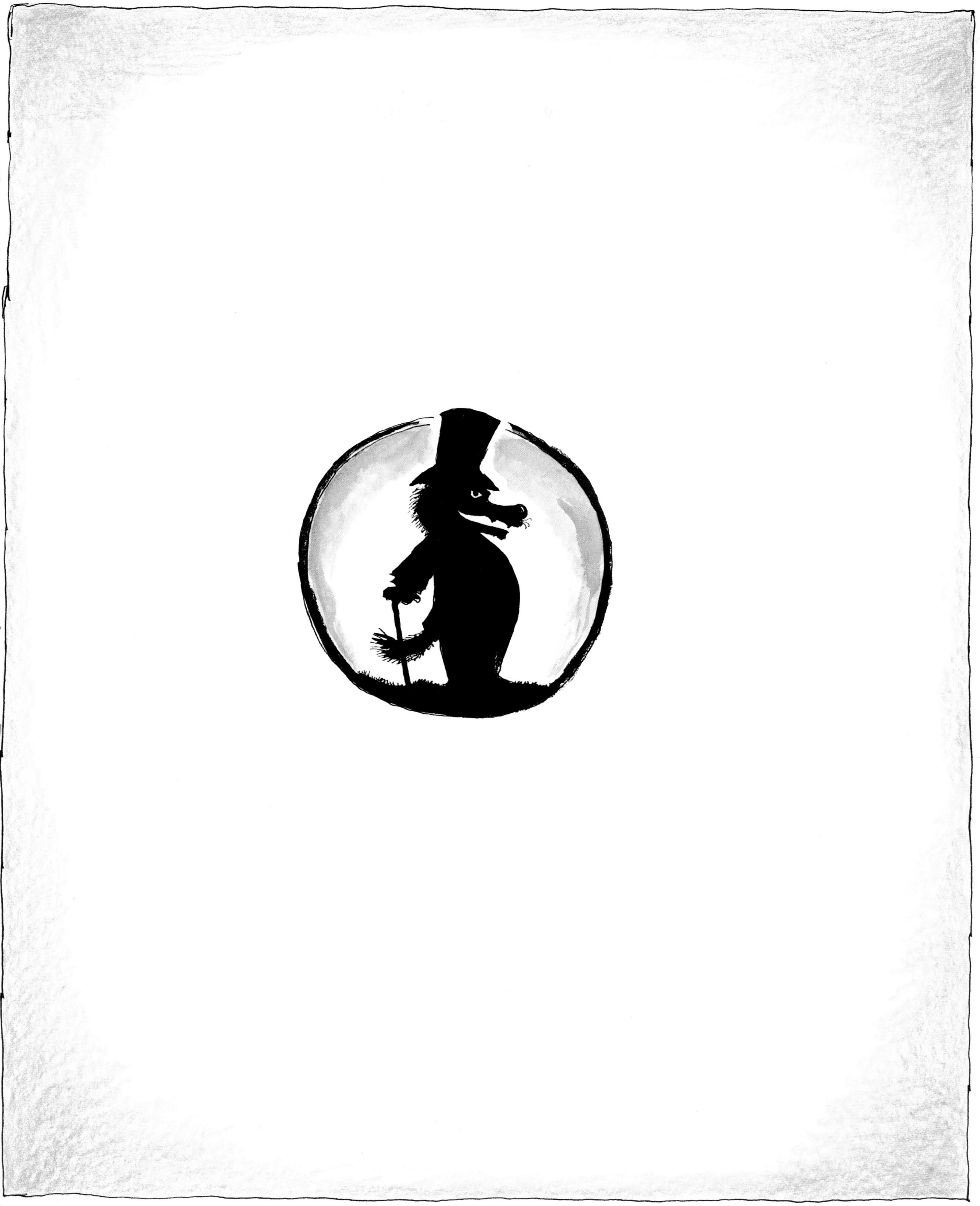

There's a Wolf at the Door

by Zoë B. Alley

pictures by R.W. Alley

A Neal Porter Book
Roaring Brook Press
New York

Text copyright © 2008 by Zoë B. Alley

Illustrations copyright © 2008 by R.W. Alley

Published by Roaring Brook Press

Roaring Brook Press is a division of Holtzbrinck Publishing Holdings Limited Partnership

175 Fifth Avenue, New York, New York 10010

www.roaringbrookpress.com

Library of Congress Cataloging-in-Publication Data

Alley, Zoë B.

There's a wolf at the door / Zoë B. Alley ; illustrated by R. W. Alley. — 1st ed.

p. cm.

"A Neal Porter book."

Summary: As his plans are spoiled over and over again, the wolf keeps trying to find his dinner,

in this retelling of five well-known stories and fables.

ISBN-13: 978-1-59643-275-8   ISBN-10: 1-59643-275-6

1. Wolves—Folklore. 2. Tales. [1. Wolves—Folklore. 2. Folklore. 3. Fables.]

I. Alley, R. W. (Robert W.), ill.   II. Title.   III. Title: There is a wolf at the door.

PZ8.1.A467Th 2008

398.2—dc22

[E]

2007044025

Roaring Brook Press books are available for special promotions and premiums.

For details, contact: Director of Special Markets, Holtzbrinck Publishers.

First edition October 2008

Book design by Jennifer Browne

Printed in China

2 4 6 8 10 9 7 5 3 1

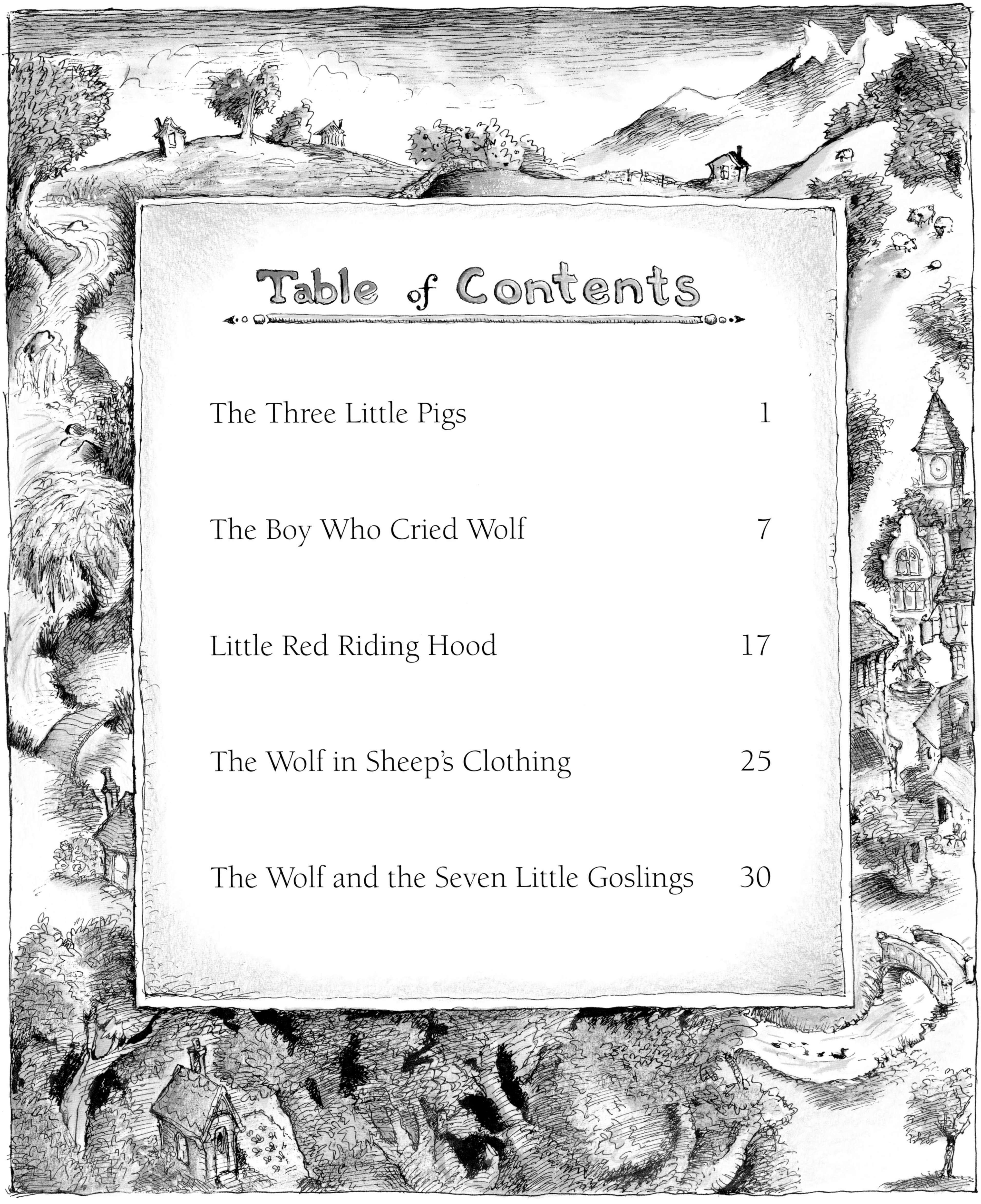

Table of Contents

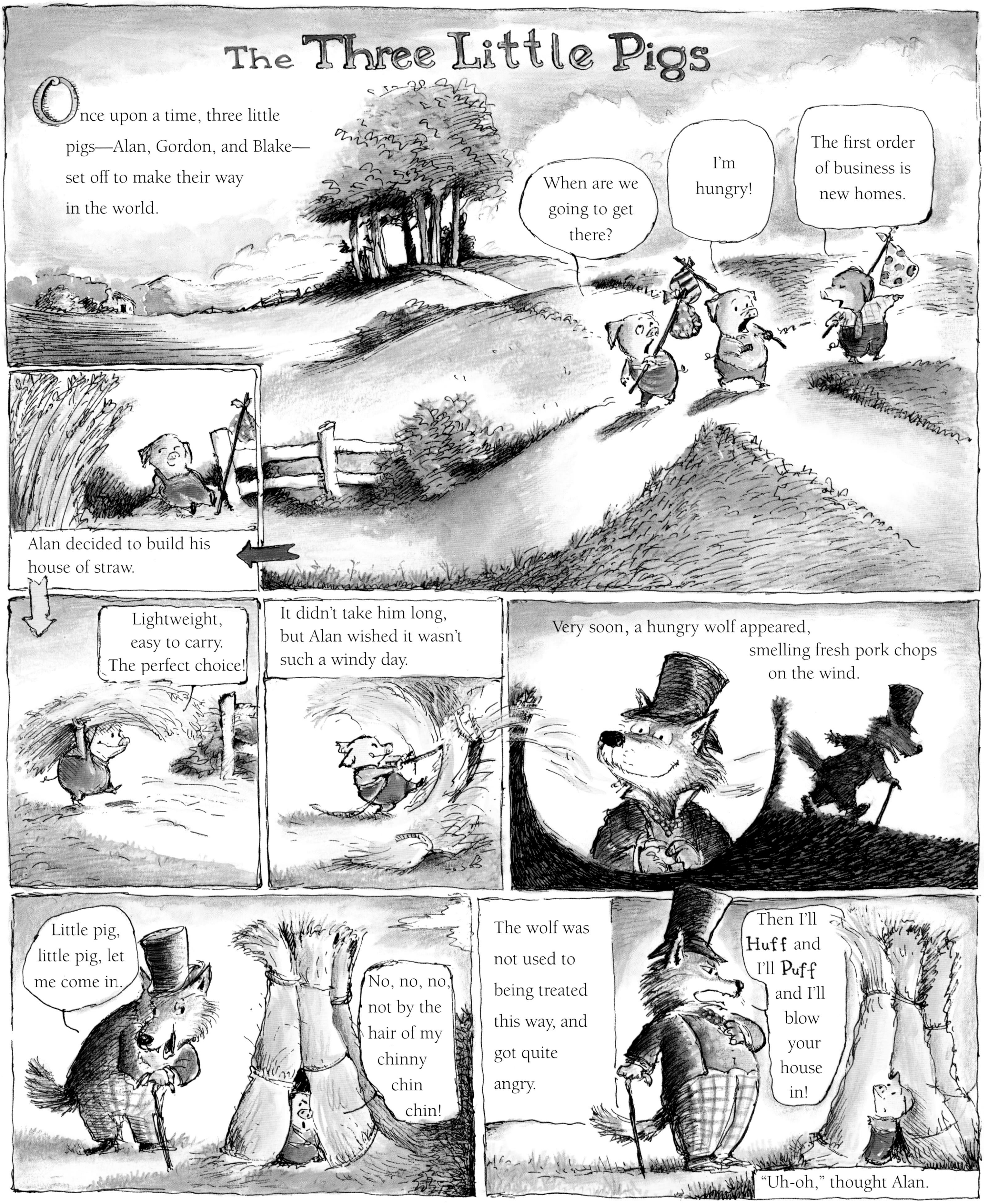
The Three Little Pigs
Once upon a time, three little pigs—Alan, Gordon, and Blake—set off to make their way in the world.
When are we going to get there?
I'm hungry!
The first order of business is new homes.
Alan decided to build his house of straw.
Lightweight, easy to carry. The perfect choice!
It didn't take him long, but Alan wished it wasn't such a windy day.
Very soon, a hungry wolf appeared, smelling fresh pork chops on the wind.
Little pig, little pig, let me come in.
No, no, no, not by the hair of my chinny chin chin!
The wolf was not used to being treated this way, and got quite angry.
Then I'll Huff and I'll Puff and I'll blow your house in!
"Uh-oh," thought Alan.

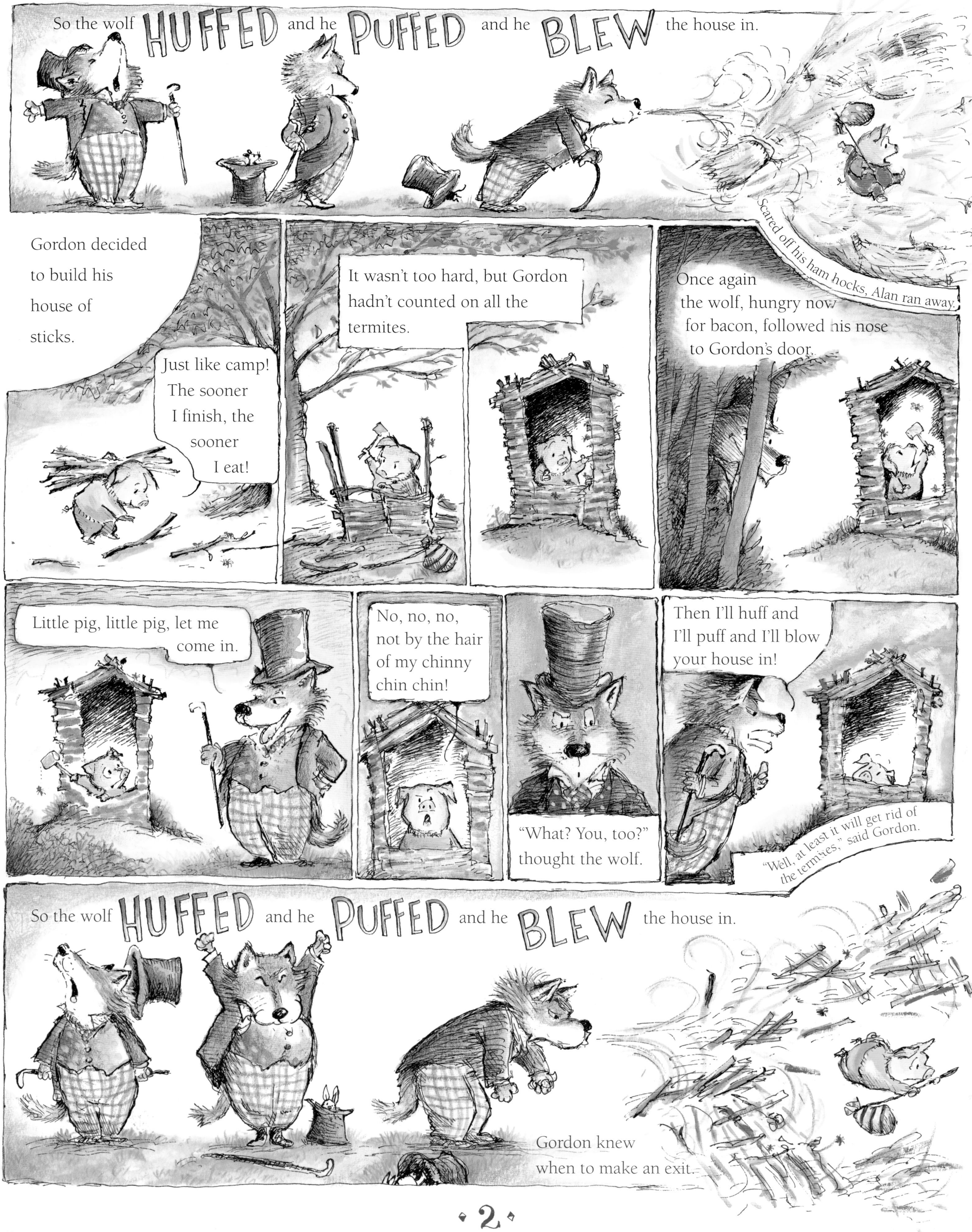
So the wolf HUFFED and he PUFFED and he BLEW the house in.
Scared off his ham hocks, Alan ran away.
Gordon decided to build his house of sticks.
Just like camp! The sooner I finish, the sooner I eat!
It wasn't too hard, but Gordon hadn't counted on all the termites.
Once again the wolf, hungry now for bacon, followed his nose to Gordon's door.
Little pig, little pig, let me come in.
No, no, no, not by the hair of my chinny chin chin!
"What? You, too?" thought the wolf.
Then I'll huff and I'll puff and I'll blow your house in!
"Well, at least it will get rid of the termites," said Gordon.
So the wolf HUFFED and he PUFFED and he BLEW the house in.
Gordon knew when to make an exit.

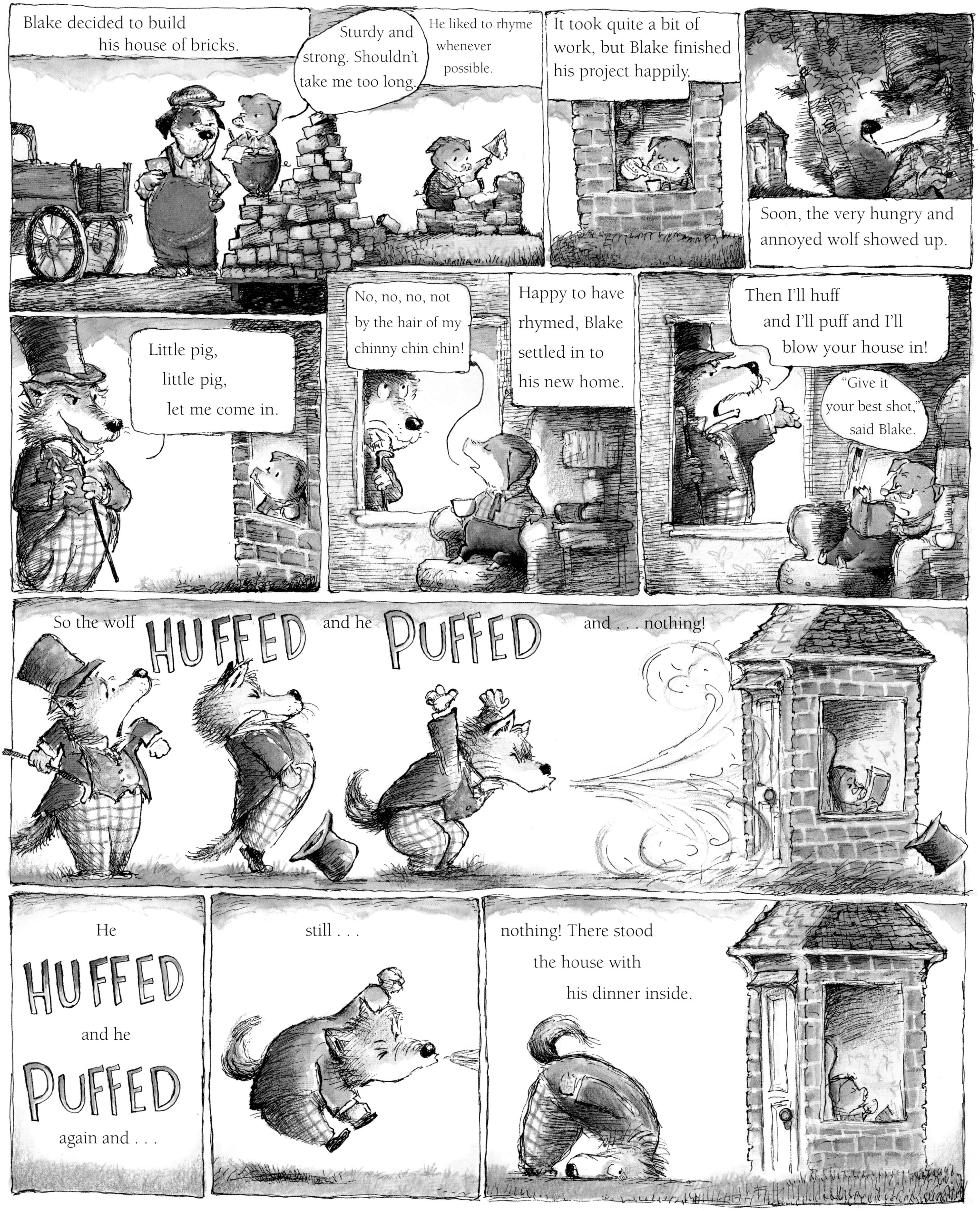
Blake decided to build his house of bricks.
Sturdy and strong. Shouldn't take me too long.
He liked to rhyme whenever possible.
It took quite a bit of work, but Blake finished his project happily.
Soon, the very hungry and annoyed wolf showed up.
Little pig, little pig, let me come in.
No, no, no, not by the hair of my chinny chin chin!
Happy to have rhymed, Blake settled in to his new home.
Then I'll huff and I'll puff and I'll blow your house in!
"Give it your best shot," said Blake.
So the wolf HUFFED and he PUFFED and . . . nothing!
He HUFFED and he PUFFED again and . . .
still . . .
nothing! There stood the house with his dinner inside.

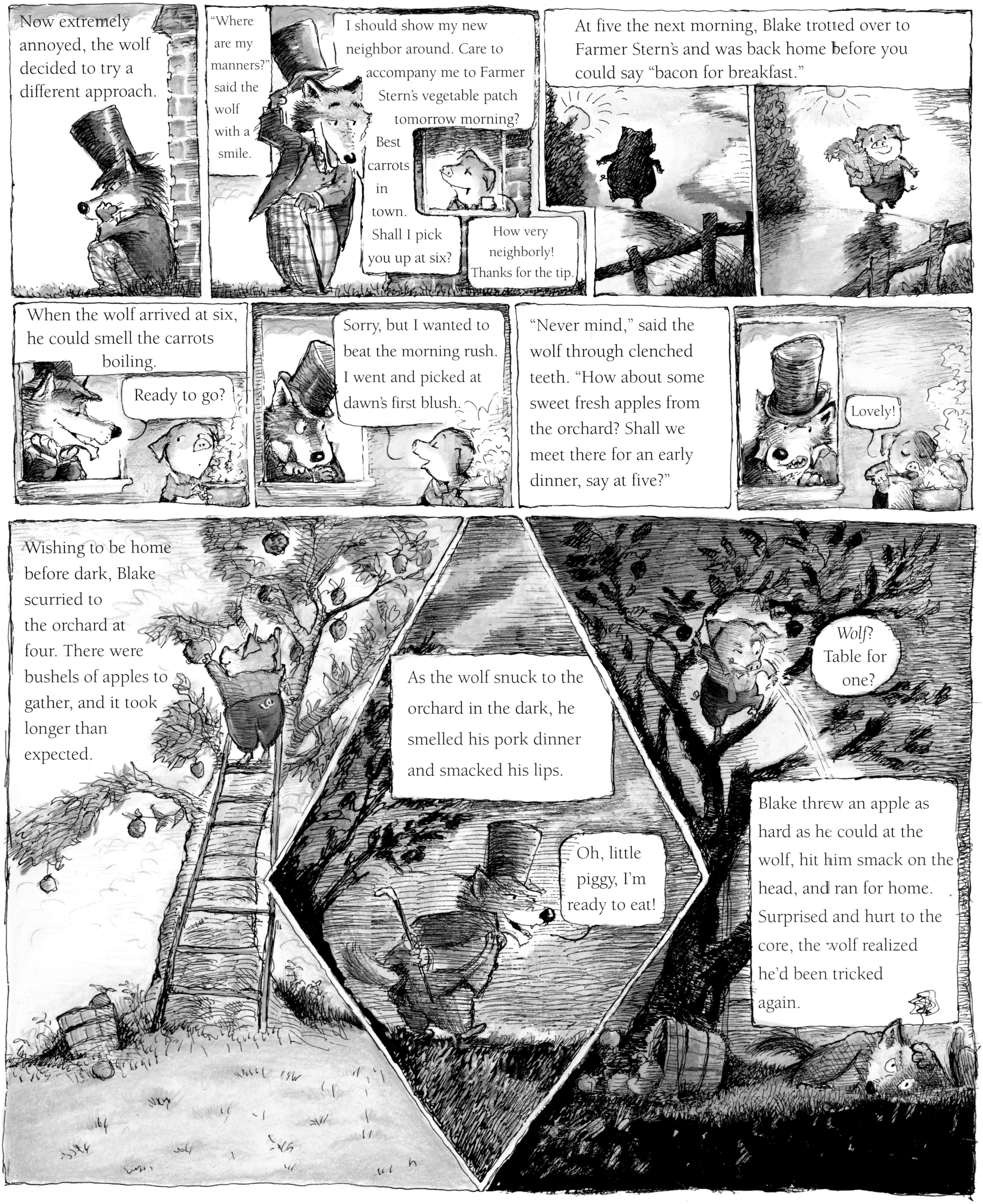
Now extremely annoyed, the wolf decided to try a different approach.
"Where are my manners?" said the wolf with a smile.
I should show my new neighbor around. Care to accompany me to Farmer Stern's vegetable patch tomorrow morning?
Best carrots in town. Shall I pick you up at six?
How very neighborly! Thanks for the tip.
At five the next morning, Blake trotted over to Farmer Stern's and was back home before you could say "bacon for breakfast."
When the wolf arrived at six, he could smell the carrots boiling.
Ready to go?
Sorry, but I wanted to beat the morning rush. I went and picked at dawn's first blush.
"Never mind," said the wolf through clenched teeth. "How about some sweet fresh apples from the orchard? Shall we meet there for an early dinner, say at five?"
Lovely!
Wishing to be home before dark, Blake scurried to the orchard at four. There were bushels of apples to gather, and it took longer than expected.
As the wolf snuck to the orchard in the dark, he smelled his pork dinner and smacked his lips.
Oh, little piggy, I'm ready to eat!
Wolf? Table for one?
Blake threw an apple as hard as he could at the wolf, hit him smack on the head, and ran for home. Surprised and hurt to the core, the wolf realized he'd been tricked again.

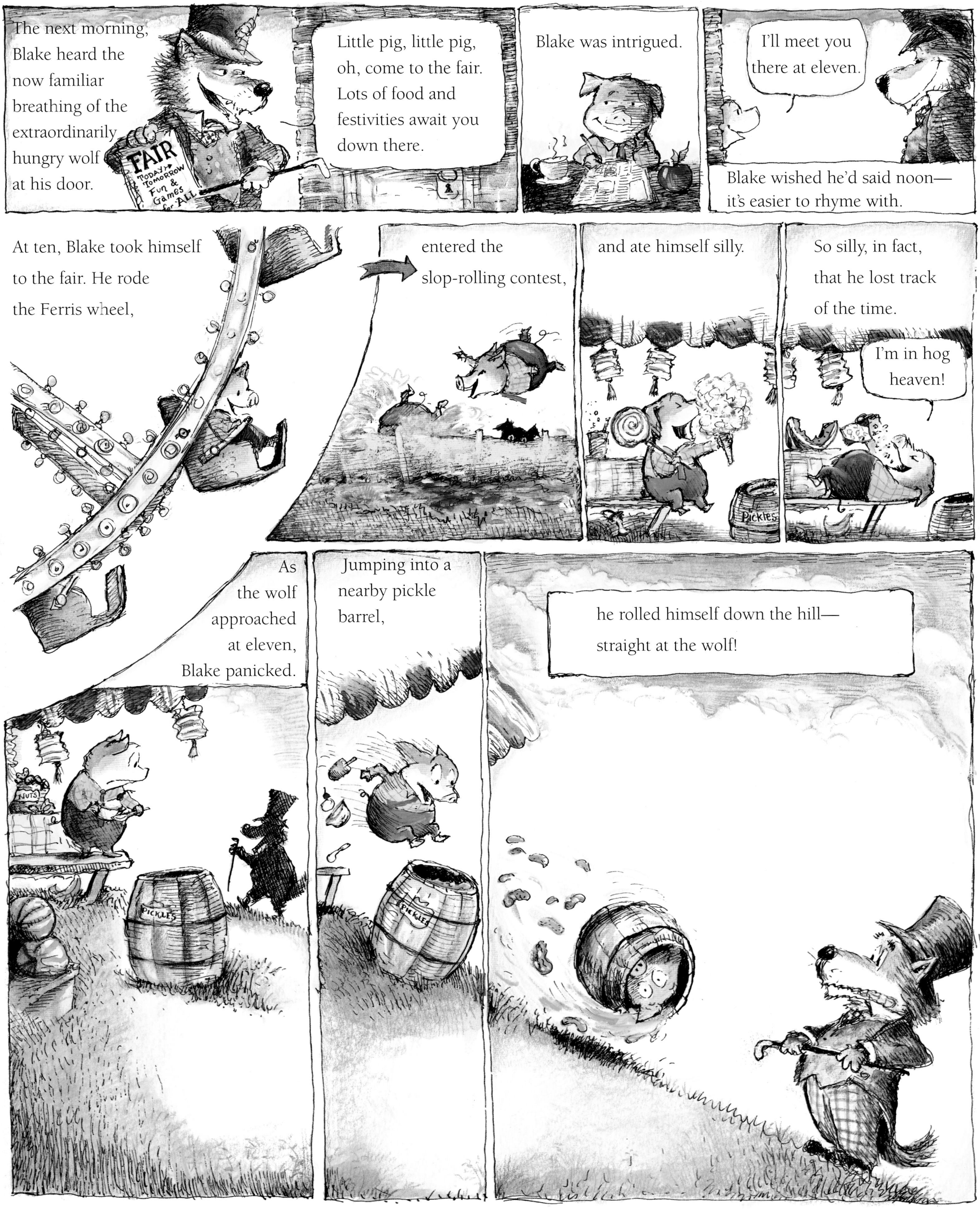
The next morning, Blake heard the now familiar breathing of the extraordinarily hungry wolf at his door.
FAIR
TODAY → TOMORROW Fun & Games for ALL
Little pig, little pig, oh, come to the fair. Lots of food and festivities await you down there.
Blake was intrigued.
I'll meet you there at eleven.
Blake wished he'd said noon—it's easier to rhyme with.
At ten, Blake took himself to the fair. He rode the Ferris wheel,
entered the slop-rolling contest,
and ate himself silly.
PICKLES
So silly, in fact, that he lost track of the time.
I'm in hog heaven!
As the wolf approached at eleven, Blake panicked.
NUTS
PICKLES
Jumping into a nearby pickle barrel,
PICKLES
he rolled himself down the hill—straight at the wolf!

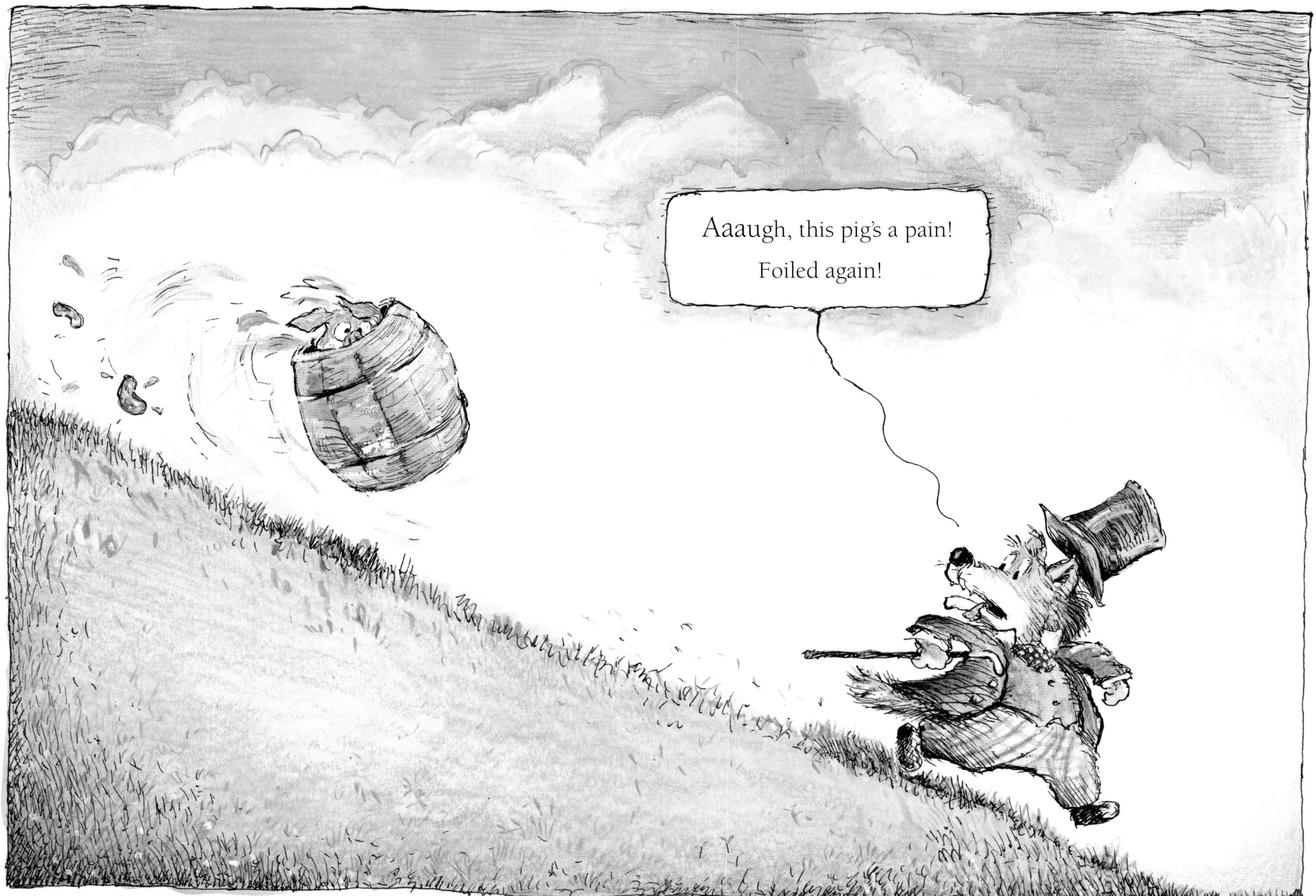
Aaaugh, this pig's a pain!
Foiled again!

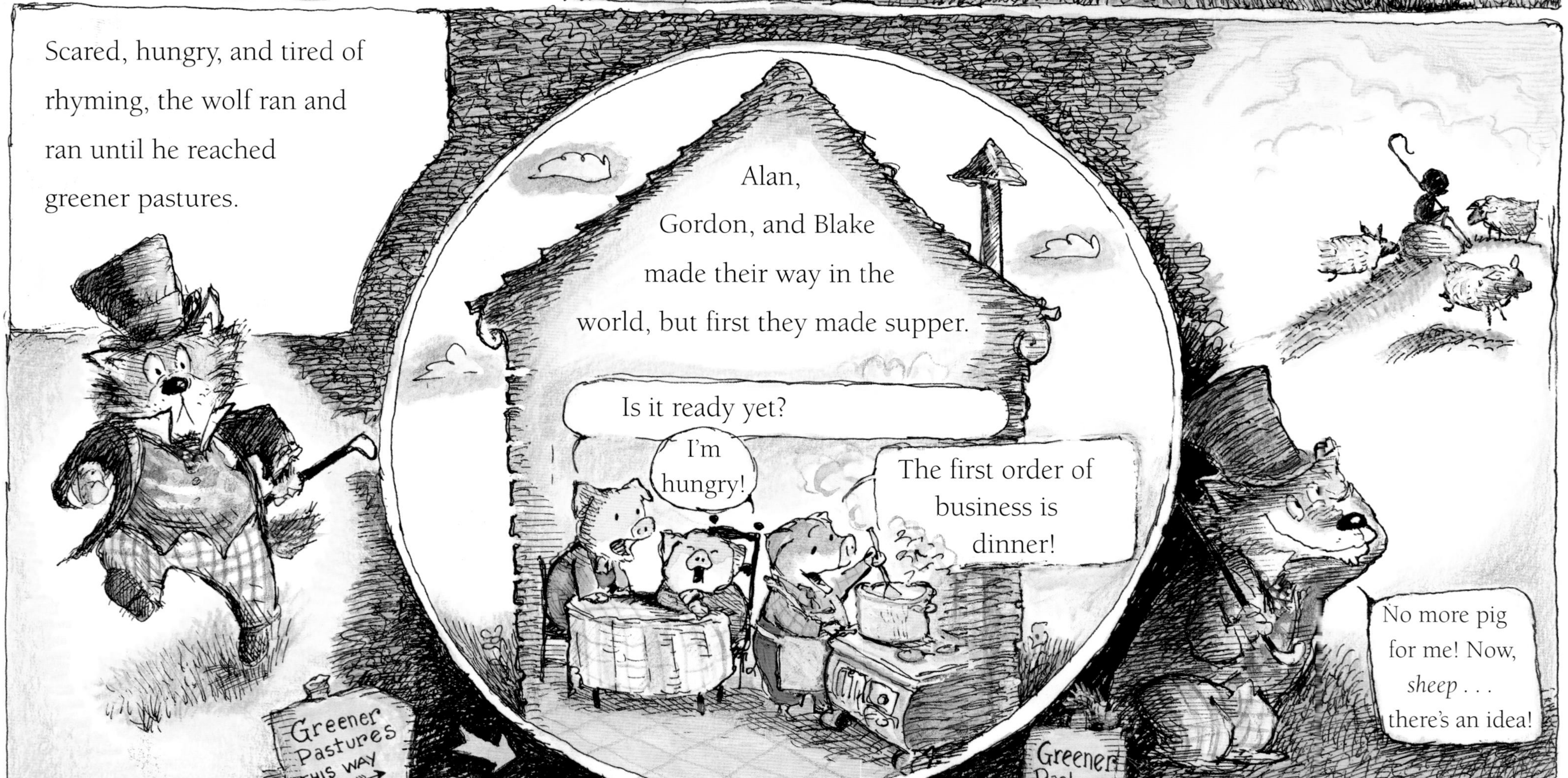
Scared, hungry, and tired of rhyming, the wolf ran and ran until he reached greener pastures.
Alan, Gordon, and Blake made their way in the world, but first they made supper.
Is it ready yet?
I'm hungry!
The first order of business is dinner!
Greener Pastures THIS WAY
Greener Pastures
No more pig for me! Now, *sheep* . . . there's an idea!

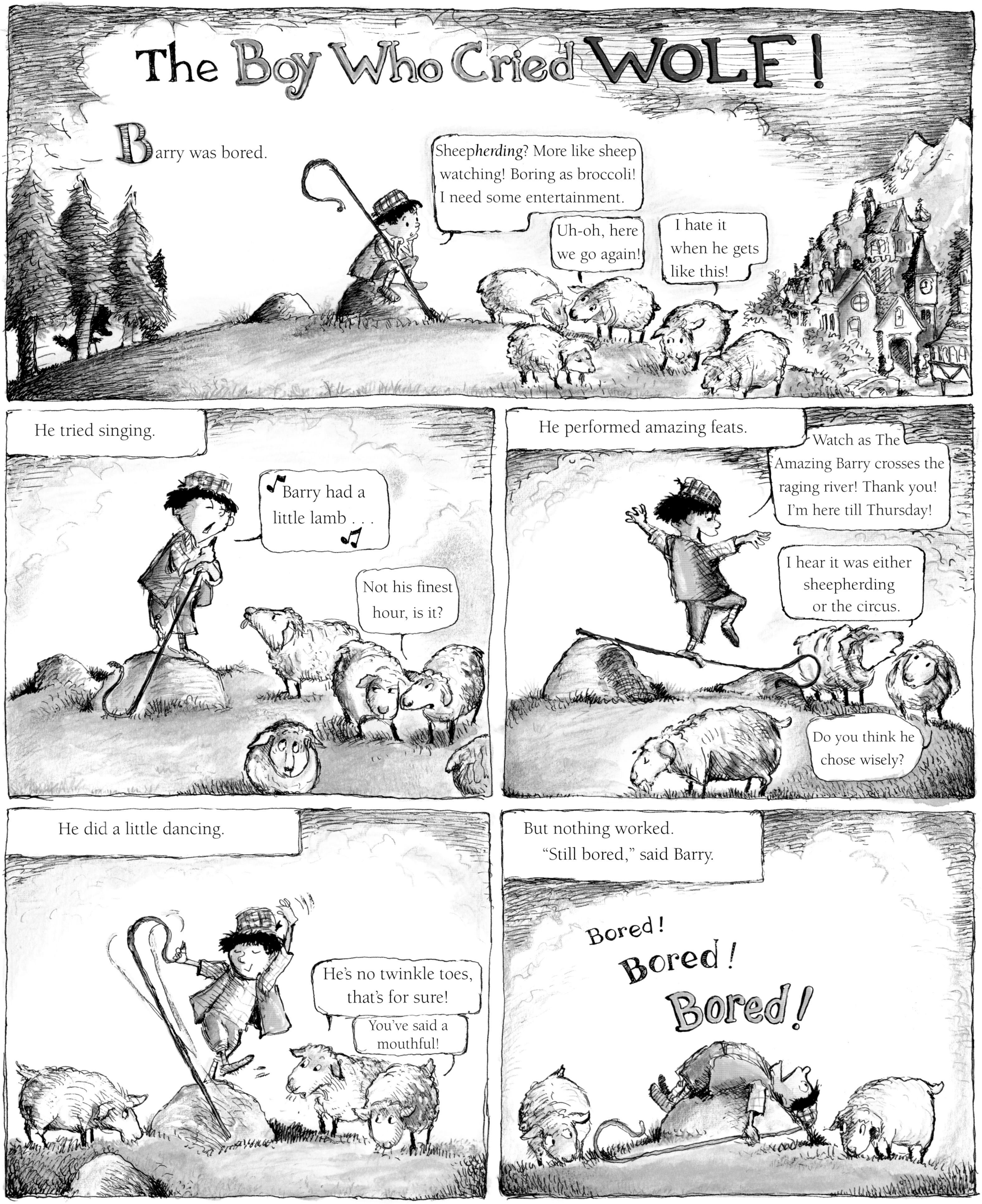
The Boy Who Cried WOLF!
Barry was bored.
Sheep*herding*? More like sheep watching! Boring as broccoli! I need some entertainment.
Uh-oh, here we go again!
I hate it when he gets like this!
He tried singing.
Barry had a little lamb . . .
Not his finest hour, is it?
He performed amazing feats.
Watch as The Amazing Barry crosses the raging river! Thank you! I'm here till Thursday!
I hear it was either sheepherding or the circus.
Do you think he chose wisely?
He did a little dancing.
He's no twinkle toes, that's for sure!
You've said a mouthful!
But nothing worked.
"Still bored," said Barry.
Bored!
Bored!
Bored!

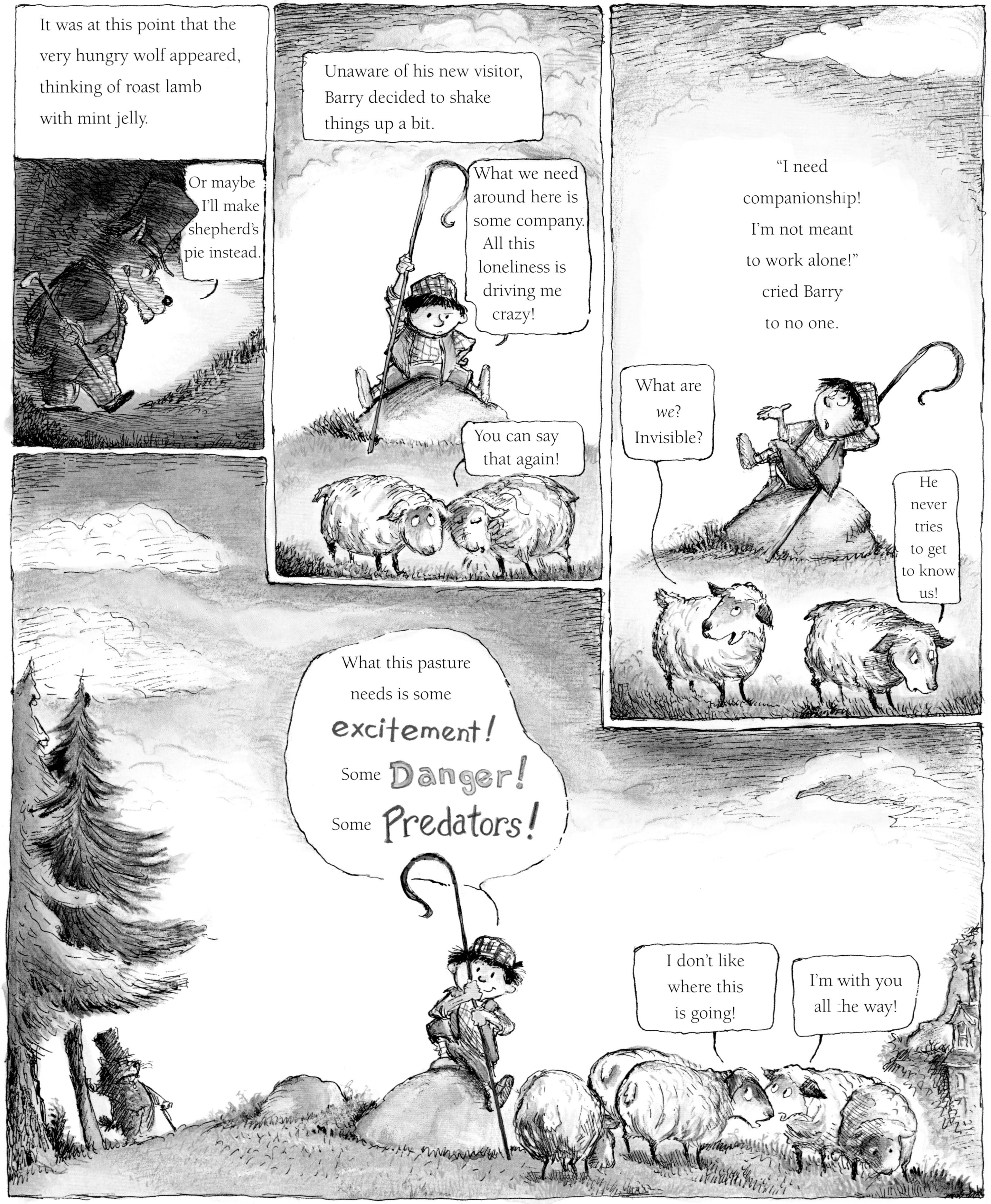
It was at this point that the very hungry wolf appeared, thinking of roast lamb with mint jelly.
Or maybe I'll make shepherd's pie instead.
Unaware of his new visitor, Barry decided to shake things up a bit.
What we need around here is some company. All this loneliness is driving me crazy!
You can say that again!
"I need companionship! I'm not meant to work alone!" cried Barry to no one.
What are *we*? Invisible?
He never tries to get to know us!
What this pasture needs is some excitement! Some Danger! Some Predators!
I don't like where this is going!
I'm with you all the way!

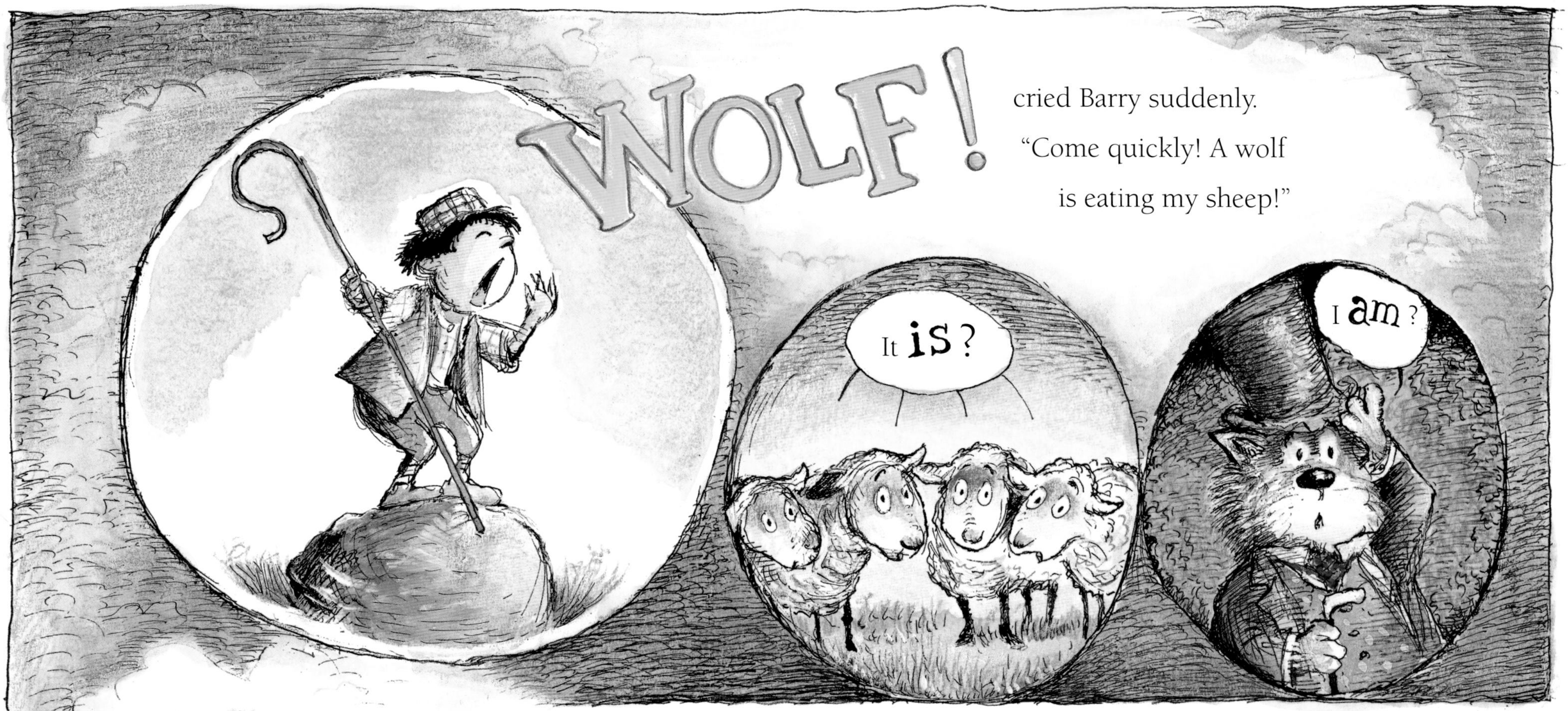
WOLF!

cried Barry suddenly. "Come quickly! A wolf is eating my sheep!"

It is?
I am?

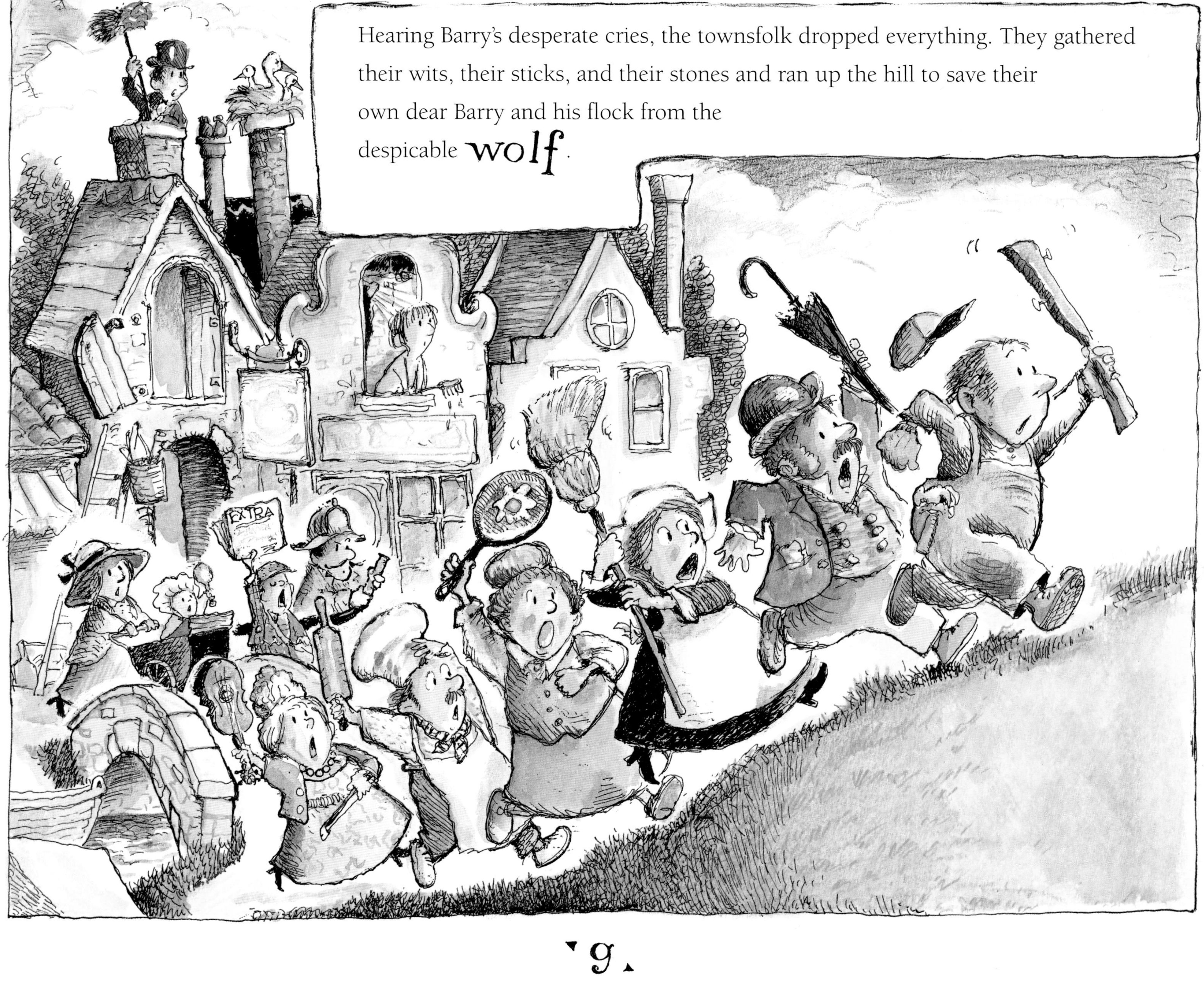
EXTRA

Hearing Barry's desperate cries, the townsfolk dropped everything. They gathered their wits, their sticks, and their stones and ran up the hill to save their own dear Barry and his flock from the despicable wolf.

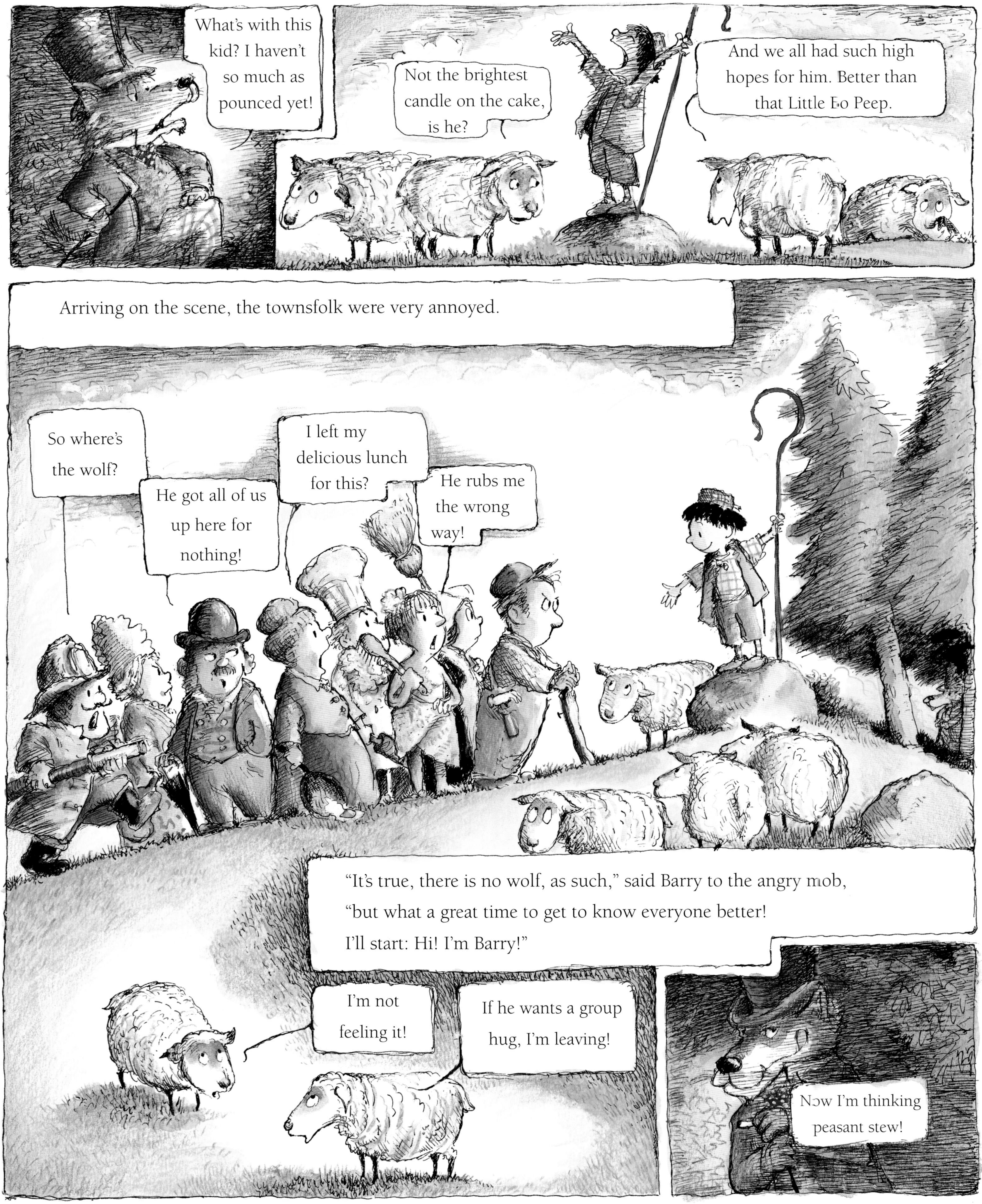
What's with this kid? I haven't so much as pounced yet!
Not the brightest candle on the cake, is he?
And we all had such high hopes for him. Better than that Little Bo Peep.
Arriving on the scene, the townsfolk were very annoyed.
So where's the wolf?
He got all of us up here for nothing!
I left my delicious lunch for this?
He rubs me the wrong way!
"It's true, there is no wolf, as such," said Barry to the angry mob, "but what a great time to get to know everyone better! I'll start: Hi! I'm Barry!"
I'm not feeling it!
If he wants a group hug, I'm leaving!
Now I'm thinking peasant stew!

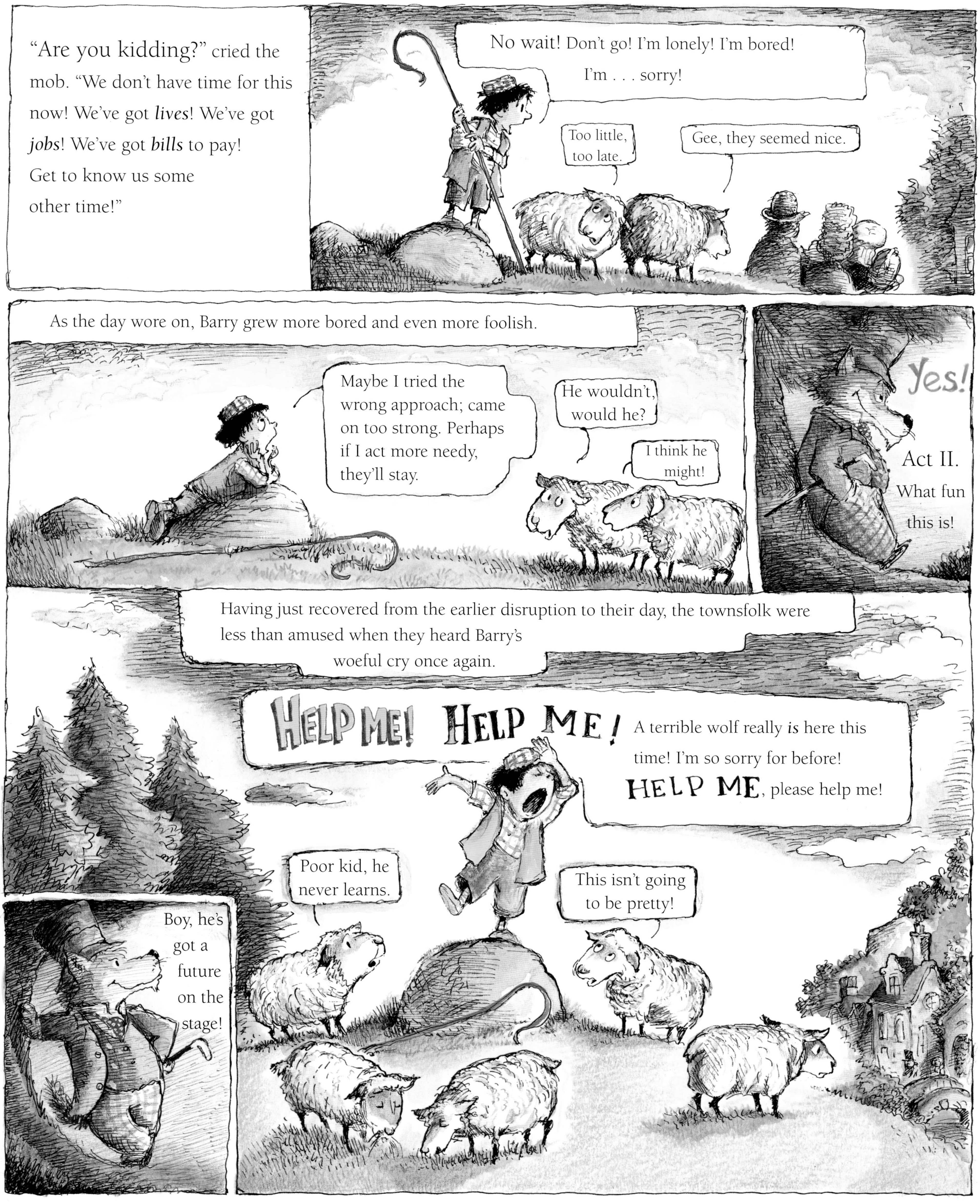

"Are you kidding?" cried the mob. "We don't have time for this now! We've got *lives*! We've got *jobs*! We've got *bills* to pay! Get to know us some other time!"
No wait! Don't go! I'm lonely! I'm bored! I'm . . . sorry!
Too little, too late.
Gee, they seemed nice.
As the day wore on, Barry grew more bored and even more foolish.
Maybe I tried the wrong approach; came on too strong. Perhaps if I act more needy, they'll stay.
He wouldn't, would he?
I think he might!
Yes!
Act II. What fun this is!
Having just recovered from the earlier disruption to their day, the townsfolk were less than amused when they heard Barry's woeful cry once again.
HELP ME! HELP ME! A terrible wolf really *is* here this time! I'm so sorry for before! HELP ME, please help me!
Poor kid, he never learns.
This isn't going to be pretty!
Boy, he's got a future on the stage!

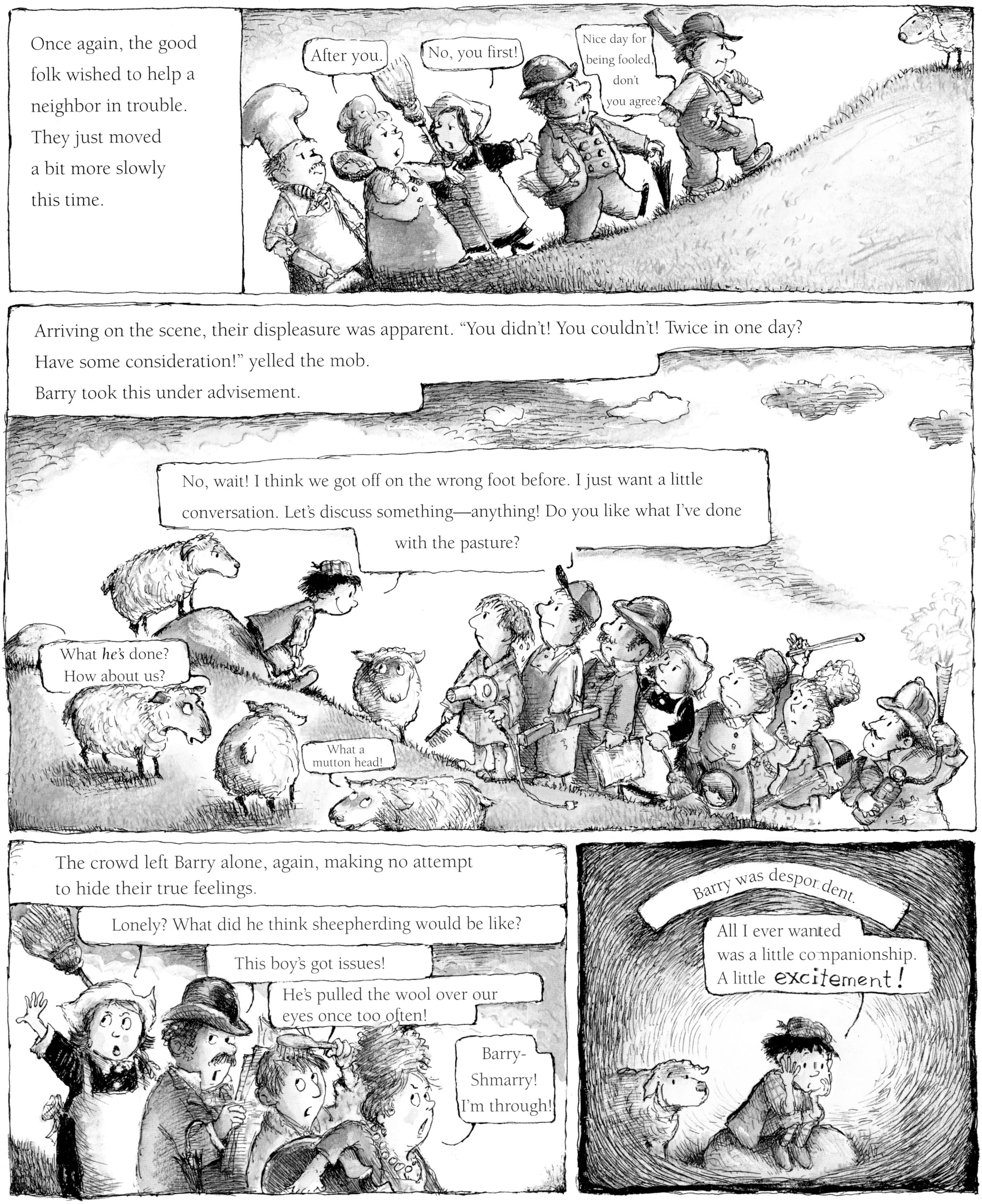
Once again, the good folk wished to help a neighbor in trouble. They just moved a bit more slowly this time.
After you.
No, you first!
Nice day for being fooled, don't you agree?
Arriving on the scene, their displeasure was apparent. "You didn't! You couldn't! Twice in one day? Have some consideration!" yelled the mob.
Barry took this under advisement.
No, wait! I think we got off on the wrong foot before. I just want a little conversation. Let's discuss something—anything! Do you like what I've done with the pasture?
What *he's* done? How about us?
What a mutton head!
The crowd left Barry alone, again, making no attempt to hide their true feelings.
Lonely? What did he think sheepherding would be like?
This boy's got issues!
He's pulled the wool over our eyes once too often!
Barry-Shmarry! I'm through!
Barry was despondent.
All I ever wanted was a little companionship. A little excitement!

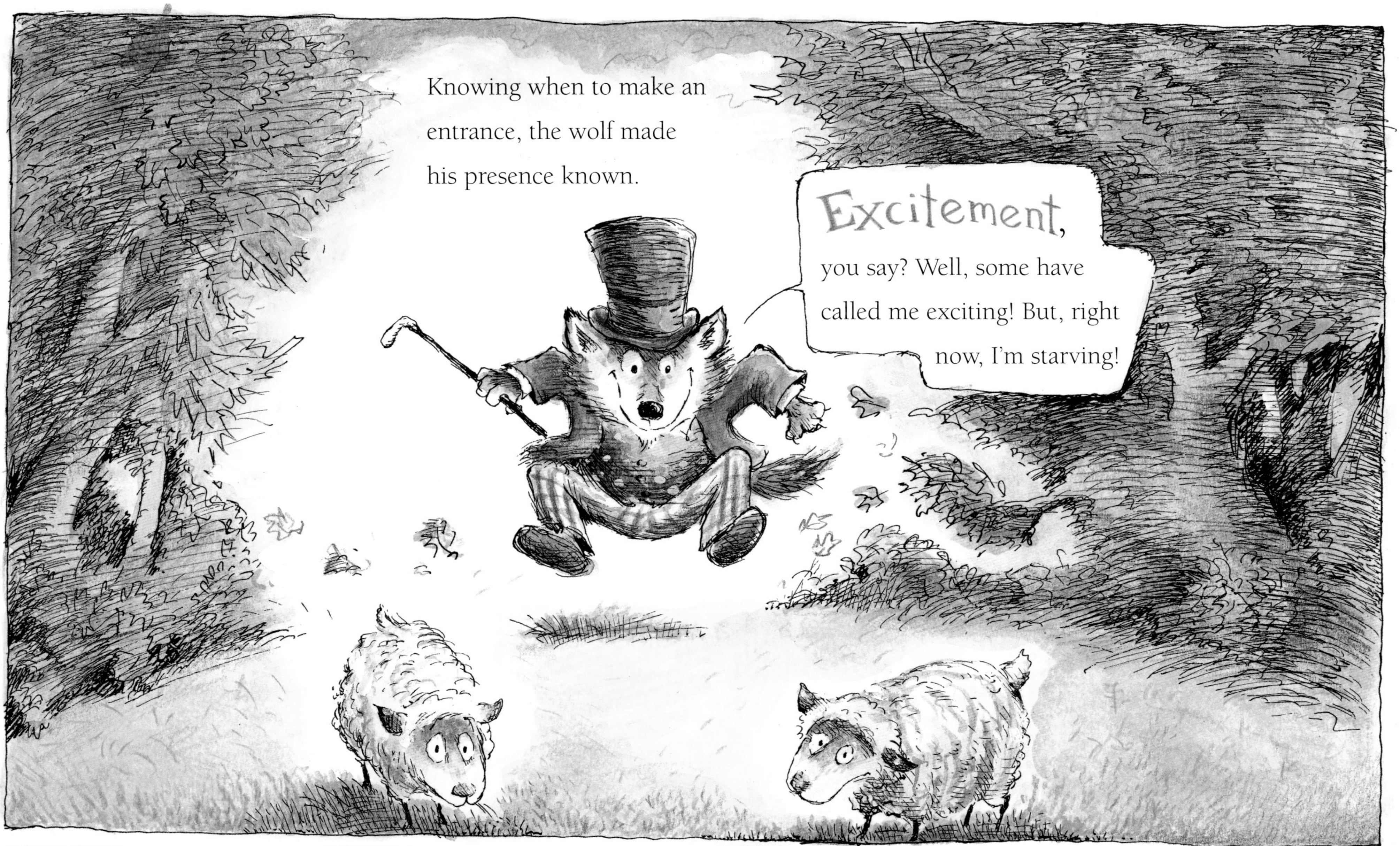
Knowing when to make an entrance, the wolf made his presence known.
Excitement, you say? Well, some have called me exciting! But, right now, I'm starving!

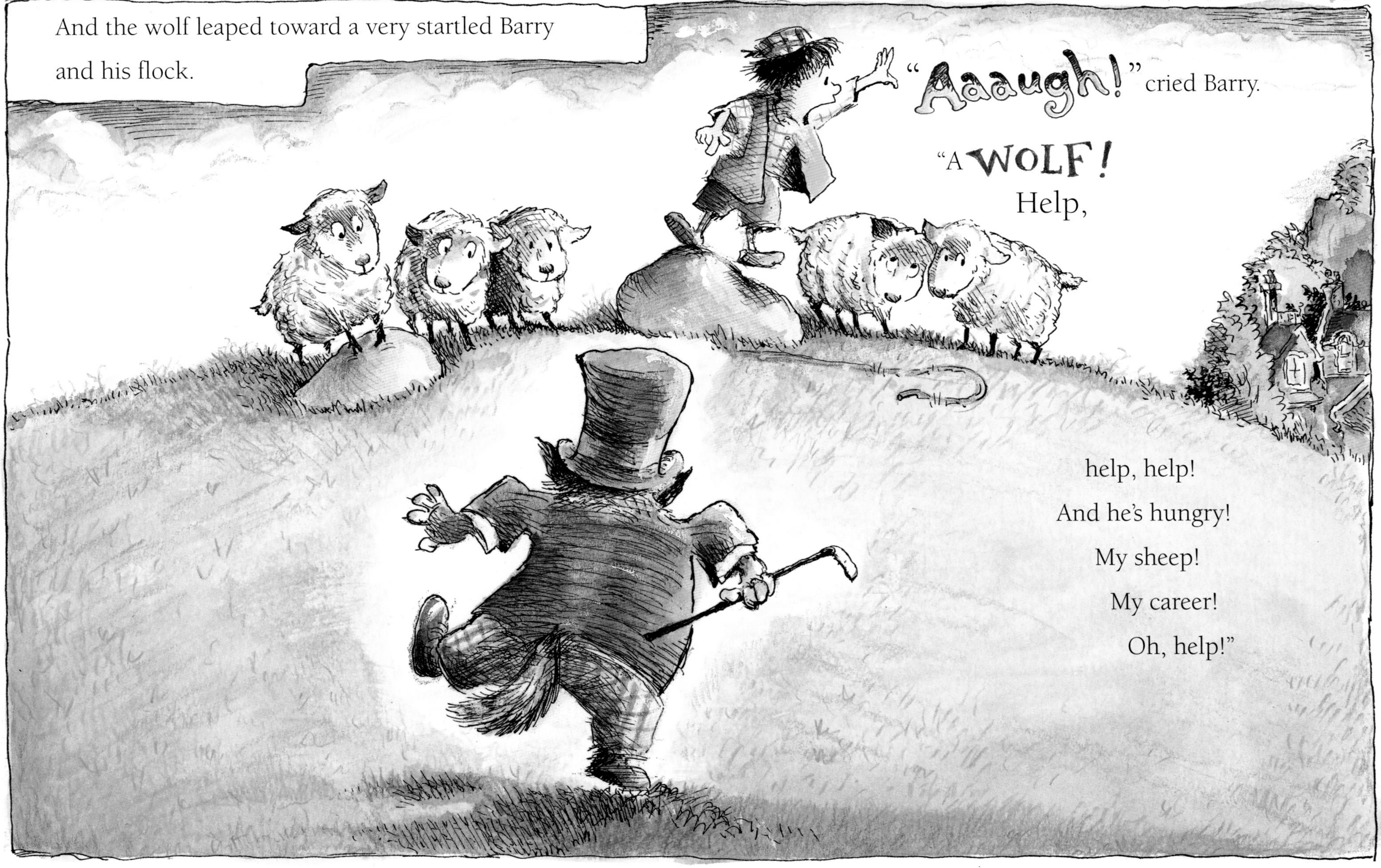
And the wolf leaped toward a very startled Barry and his flock.
"Aaaugh!" cried Barry.
"A WOLF! Help, help, help! And he's hungry! My sheep! My career! Oh, help!"

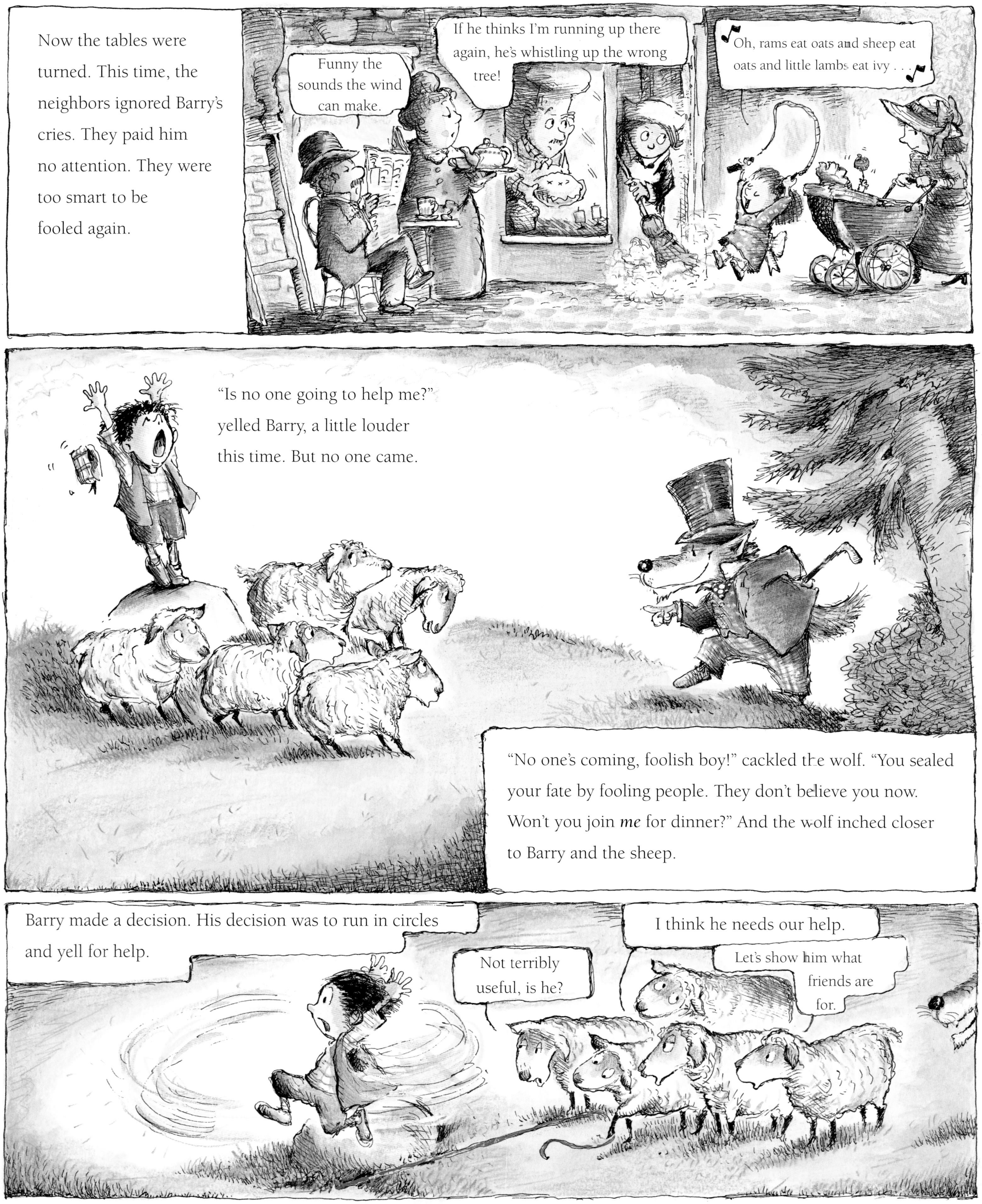
Now the tables were turned. This time, the neighbors ignored Barry's cries. They paid him no attention. They were too smart to be fooled again.
Funny the sounds the wind can make.
If he thinks I'm running up there again, he's whistling up the wrong tree!
Oh, rams eat oats and sheep eat oats and little lambs eat ivy . . .
"Is no one going to help me?" yelled Barry, a little louder this time. But no one came.
"No one's coming, foolish boy!" cackled the wolf. "You sealed your fate by fooling people. They don't believe you now. Won't you join *me* for dinner?" And the wolf inched closer to Barry and the sheep.
Barry made a decision. His decision was to run in circles and yell for help.
Not terribly useful, is he?
I think he needs our help.
Let's show him what friends are for.

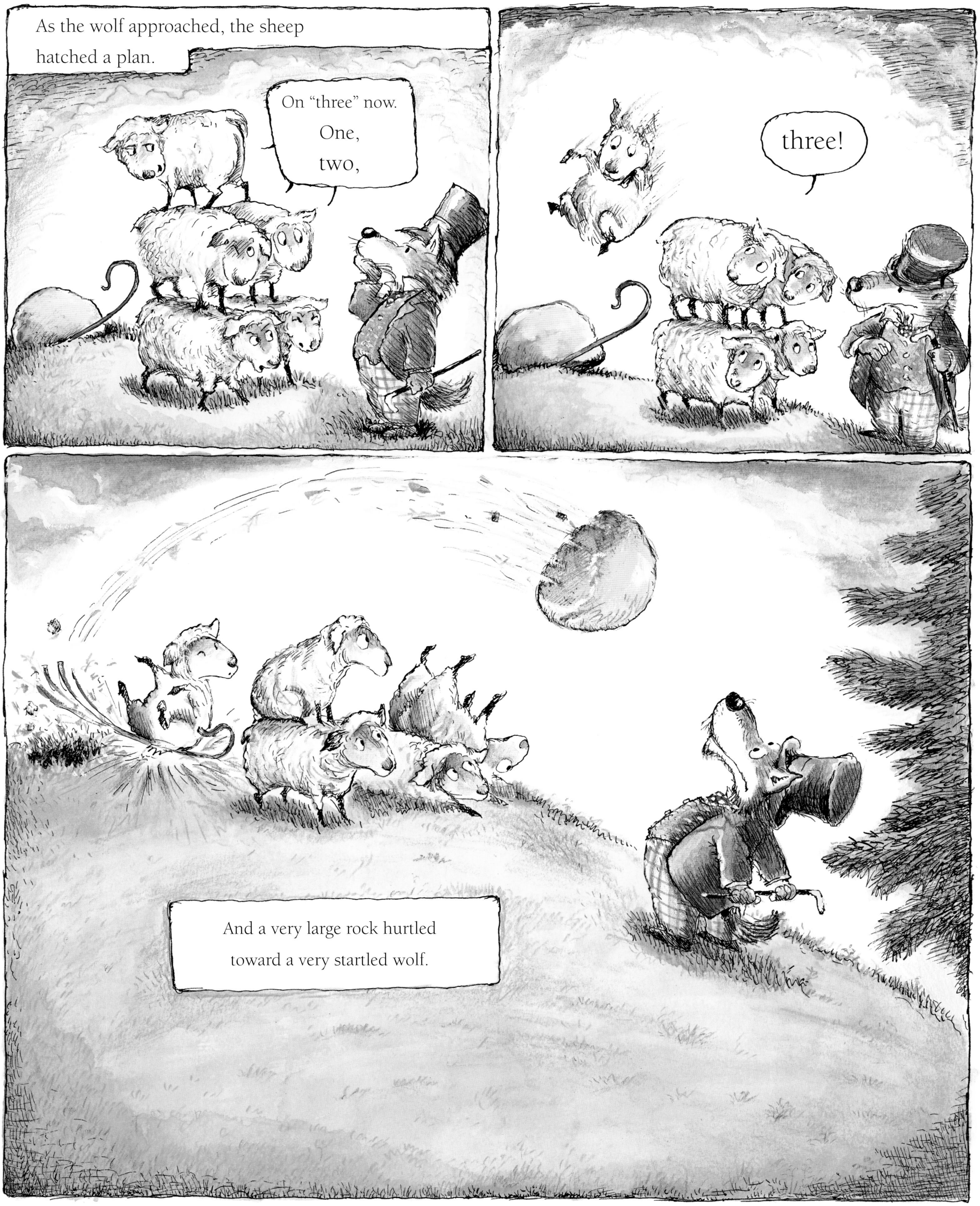
As the wolf approached, the sheep hatched a plan.
On "three" now. One, two,
three!
And a very large rock hurtled toward a very startled wolf.

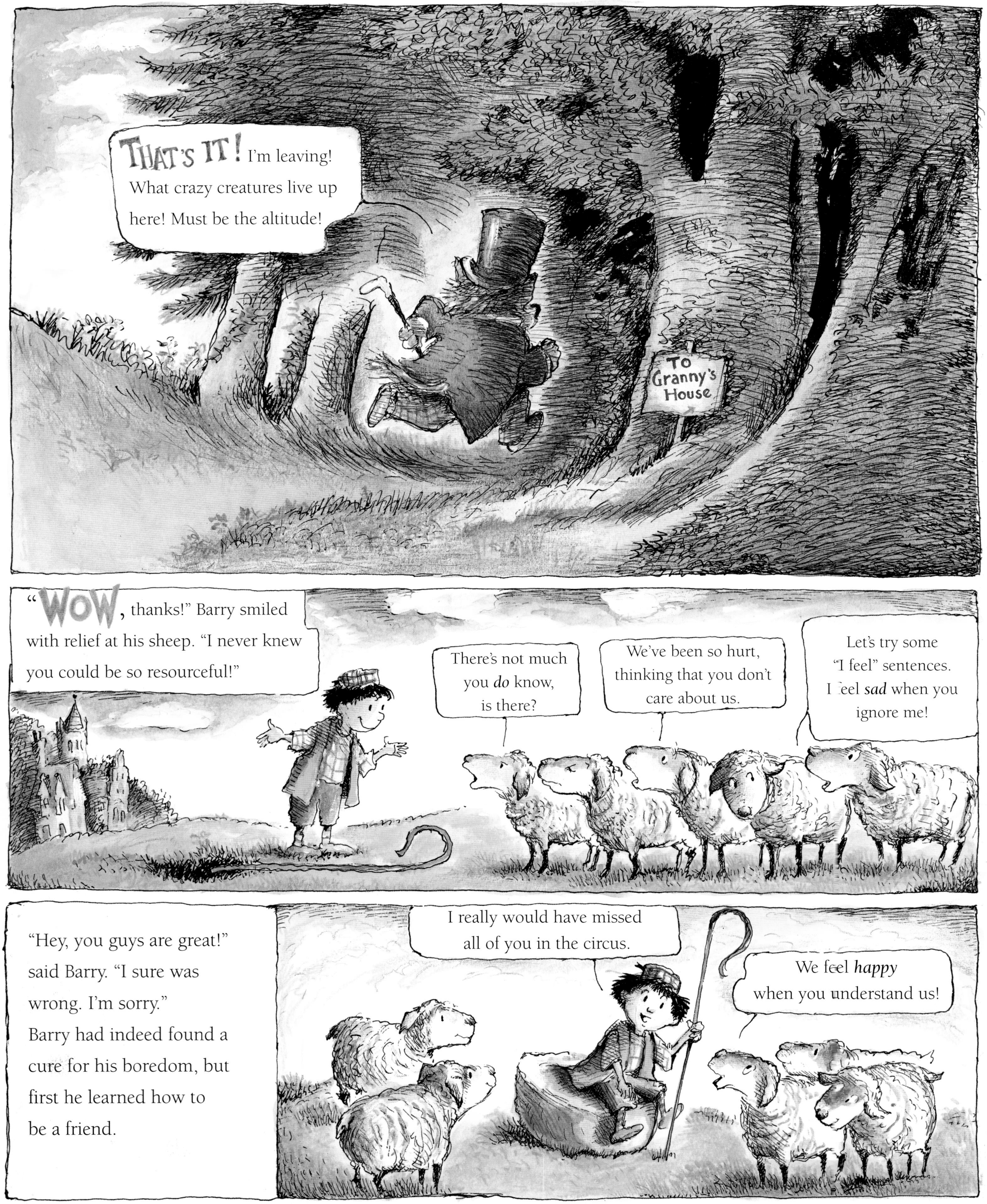
THAT'S IT! I'm leaving! What crazy creatures live up here! Must be the altitude!
To Granny's House
"WOW, thanks!" Barry smiled with relief at his sheep. "I never knew you could be so resourceful!"
There's not much you do know, is there?
We've been so hurt, thinking that you don't care about us.
Let's try some "I feel" sentences. I feel sad when you ignore me!
"Hey, you guys are great!" said Barry. "I sure was wrong. I'm sorry." Barry had indeed found a cure for his boredom, but first he learned how to be a friend.
I really would have missed all of you in the circus.
We feel happy when you understand us!

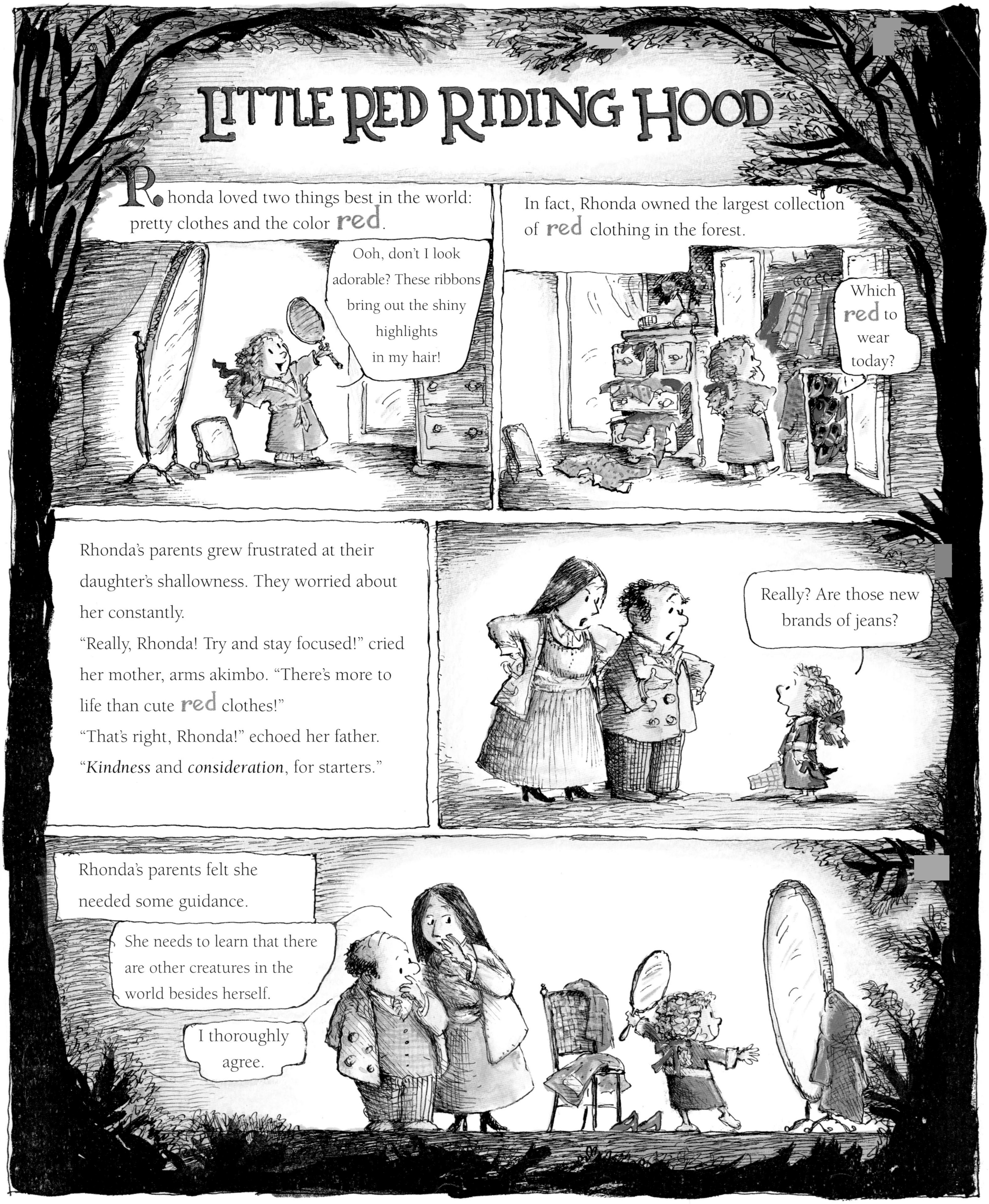
LITTLE RED RIDING HOOD
Rhonda loved two things best in the world: pretty clothes and the color red.
Ooh, don't I look adorable? These ribbons bring out the shiny highlights in my hair!
In fact, Rhonda owned the largest collection of red clothing in the forest.
Which red to wear today?
Rhonda's parents grew frustrated at their daughter's shallowness. They worried about her constantly.
"Really, Rhonda! Try and stay focused!" cried her mother, arms akimbo. "There's more to life than cute red clothes!"
"That's right, Rhonda!" echoed her father. "*Kindness* and *consideration*, for starters."
Really? Are those new brands of jeans?
Rhonda's parents felt she needed some guidance.
She needs to learn that there are other creatures in the world besides herself.
I thoroughly agree.

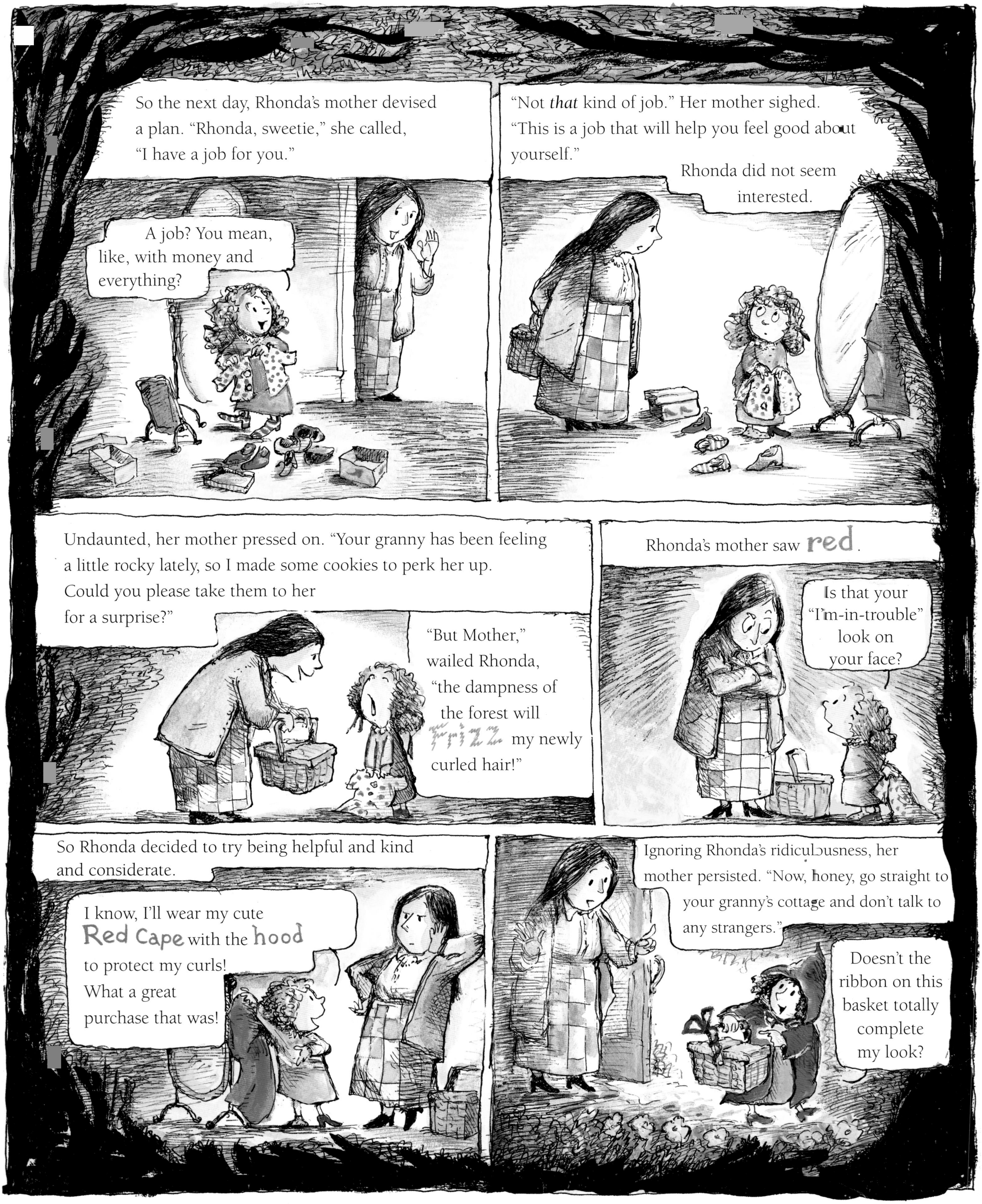
So the next day, Rhonda's mother devised a plan. "Rhonda, sweetie," she called, "I have a job for you."
A job? You mean, like, with money and everything?
"Not *that* kind of job." Her mother sighed. "This is a job that will help you feel good about yourself."
Rhonda did not seem interested.
Undaunted, her mother pressed on. "Your granny has been feeling a little rocky lately, so I made some cookies to perk her up. Could you please take them to her for a surprise?"
"But Mother," wailed Rhonda, "the dampness of the forest will frizz my newly curled hair!"
Rhonda's mother saw red.
Is that your "I'm-in-trouble" look on your face?
So Rhonda decided to try being helpful and kind and considerate.
I know, I'll wear my cute Red Cape with the hood to protect my curls! What a great purchase that was!
Ignoring Rhonda's ridiculousness, her mother persisted. "Now, honey, go straight to your granny's cottage and don't talk to any strangers."
Doesn't the ribbon on this basket totally complete my look?

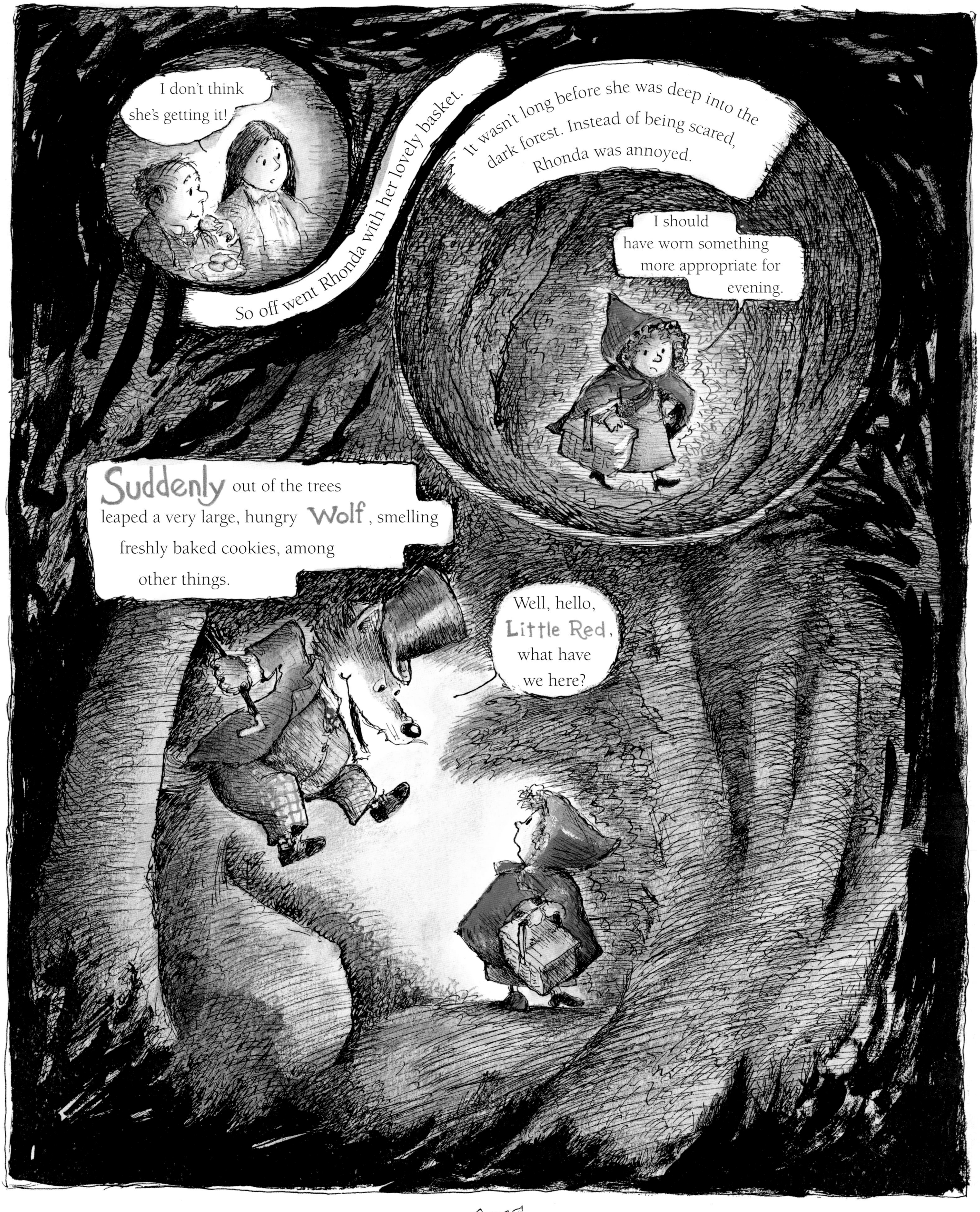

I don't think she's getting it!
So off went Rhonda with her lovely basket.
It wasn't long before she was deep into the dark forest. Instead of being scared, Rhonda was annoyed.
I should have worn something more appropriate for evening.
Suddenly out of the trees leaped a very large, hungry Wolf, smelling freshly baked cookies, among other things.
Well, hello, Little Red, what have we here?

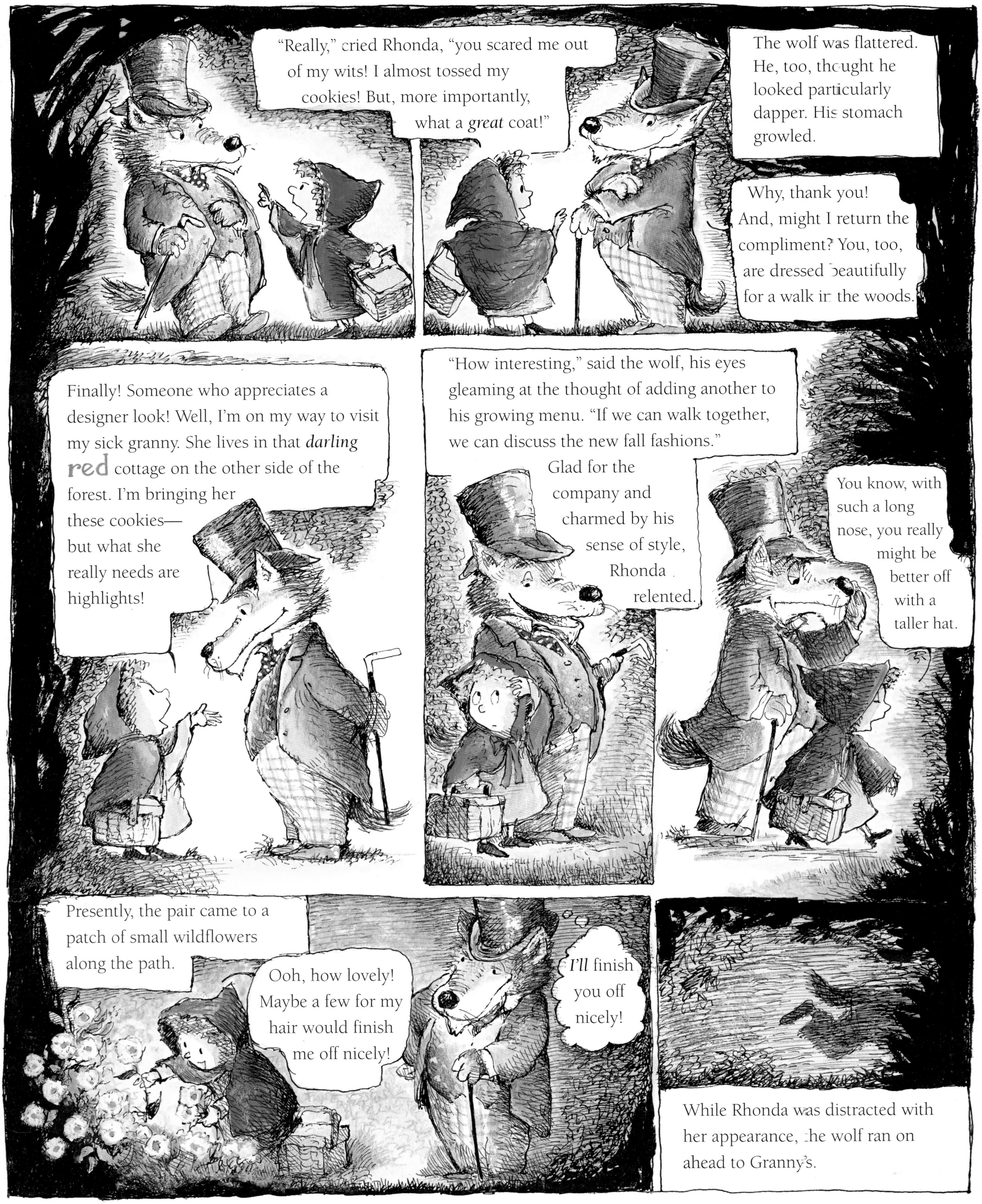
"Really," cried Rhonda, "you scared me out of my wits! I almost tossed my cookies! But, more importantly, what a *great* coat!"
The wolf was flattered. He, too, thought he looked particularly dapper. His stomach growled.
Why, thank you! And, might I return the compliment? You, too, are dressed beautifully for a walk in the woods.
Finally! Someone who appreciates a designer look! Well, I'm on my way to visit my sick granny. She lives in that *darling* red cottage on the other side of the forest. I'm bringing her these cookies—but what she really needs are highlights!
"How interesting," said the wolf, his eyes gleaming at the thought of adding another to his growing menu. "If we can walk together, we can discuss the new fall fashions."
Glad for the company and charmed by his sense of style, Rhonda relented.
You know, with such a long nose, you really might be better off with a taller hat.
Presently, the pair came to a patch of small wildflowers along the path.
Ooh, how lovely! Maybe a few for my hair would finish me off nicely!
I'll finish you off nicely!
While Rhonda was distracted with her appearance, the wolf ran on ahead to Granny's.

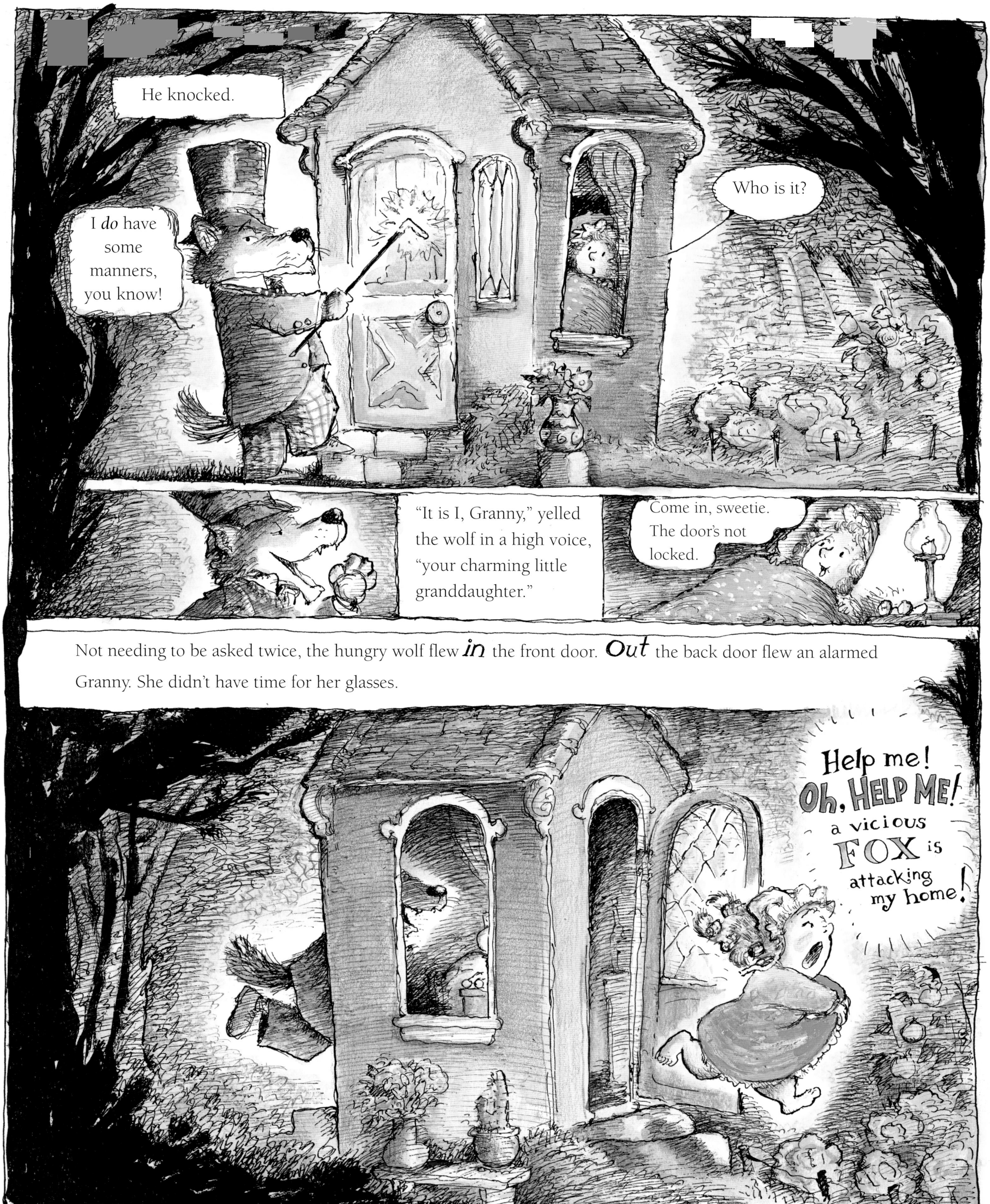
He knocked.
I *do* have some manners, you know!
Who is it?
"It is I, Granny," yelled the wolf in a high voice, "your charming little granddaughter."
Come in, sweetie. The door's not locked.
Not needing to be asked twice, the hungry wolf flew *in* the front door. *Out* the back door flew an alarmed Granny. She didn't have time for her glasses.
Help me! Oh, HELP ME! a vicious FOX is attacking my home!

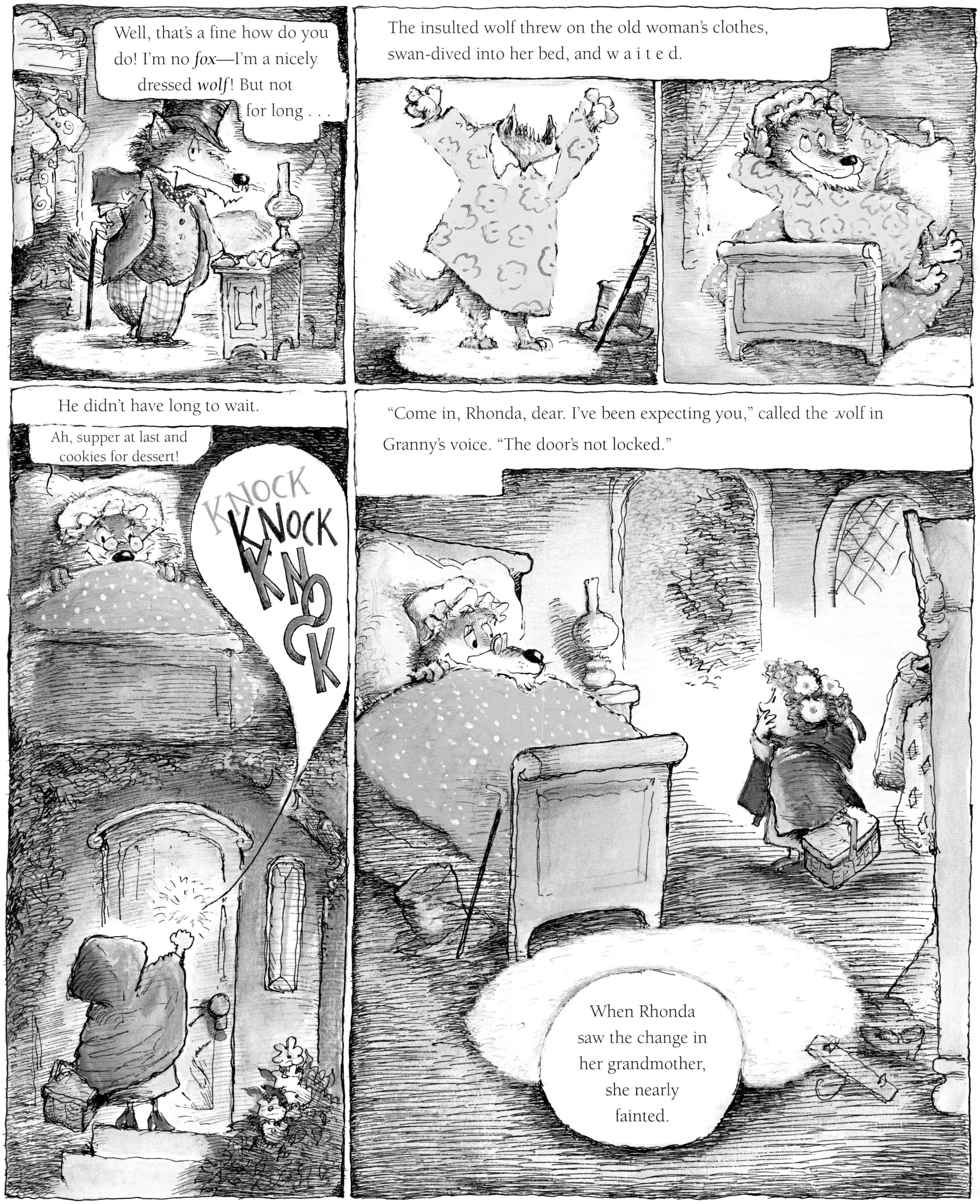
Well, that's a fine how do you do! I'm no *fox*—I'm a nicely dressed *wolf*! But not for long . . .
The insulted wolf threw on the old woman's clothes, swan-dived into her bed, and w a i t e d.
He didn't have long to wait.
Ah, supper at last and cookies for dessert!
KNOCK
KNOCK
KNOCK
"Come in, Rhonda, dear. I've been expecting you," called the wolf in Granny's voice. "The door's not locked."
When Rhonda saw the change in her grandmother, she nearly fainted.

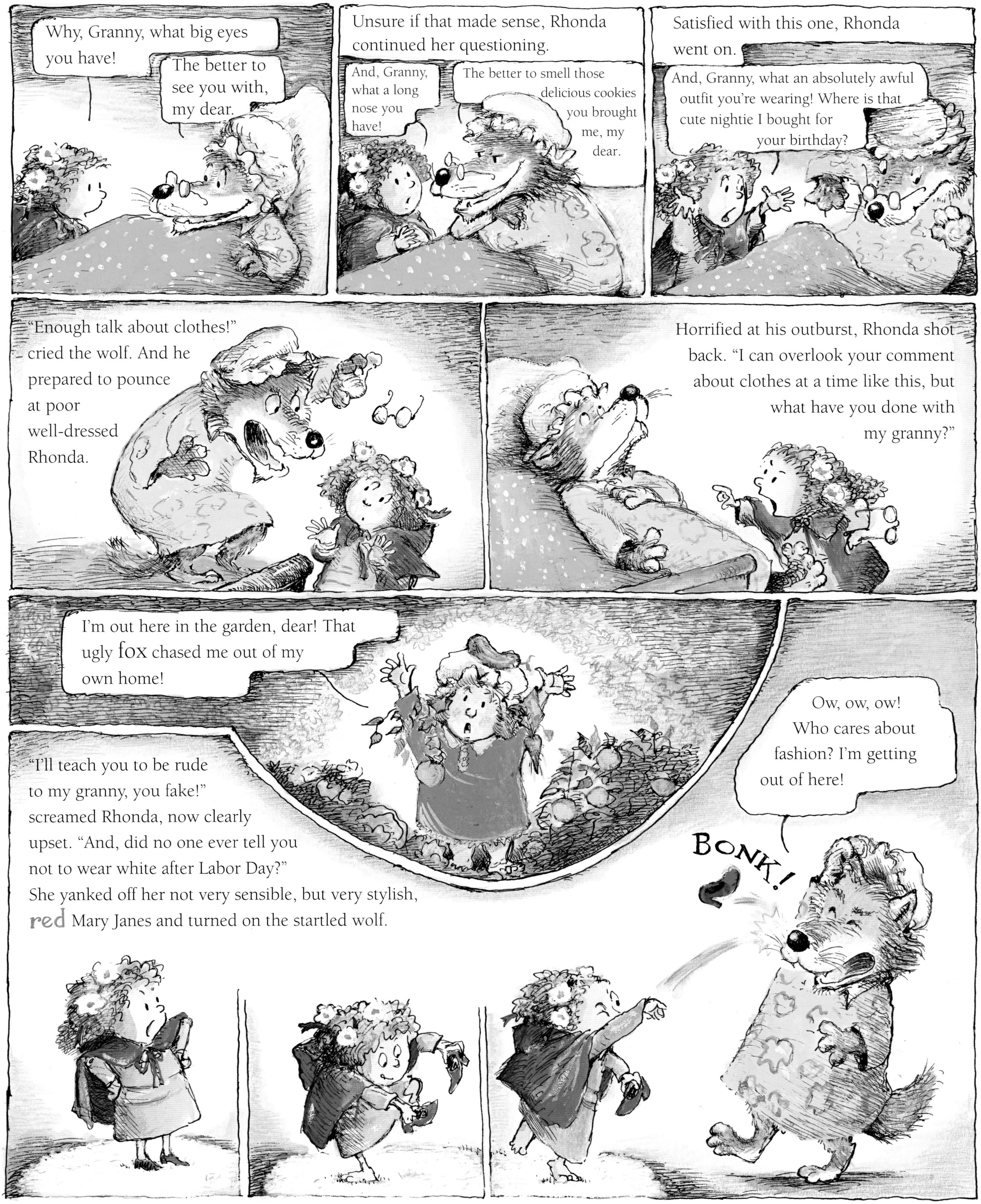
Why, Granny, what big eyes you have!
The better to see you with, my dear.
Unsure if that made sense, Rhonda continued her questioning.
And, Granny, what a long nose you have!
The better to smell those delicious cookies you brought me, my dear.
Satisfied with this one, Rhonda went on.
And, Granny, what an absolutely awful outfit you're wearing! Where is that cute nightie I bought for your birthday?
"Enough talk about clothes!" cried the wolf. And he prepared to pounce at poor well-dressed Rhonda.
Horrified at his outburst, Rhonda shot back. "I can overlook your comment about clothes at a time like this, but what have you done with my granny?"
I'm out here in the garden, dear! That ugly fox chased me out of my own home!
"I'll teach you to be rude to my granny, you fake!" screamed Rhonda, now clearly upset. "And, did no one ever tell you not to wear white after Labor Day?" She yanked off her not very sensible, but very stylish, red Mary Janes and turned on the startled wolf.
Ow, ow, ow! Who cares about fashion? I'm getting out of here!
BONK!

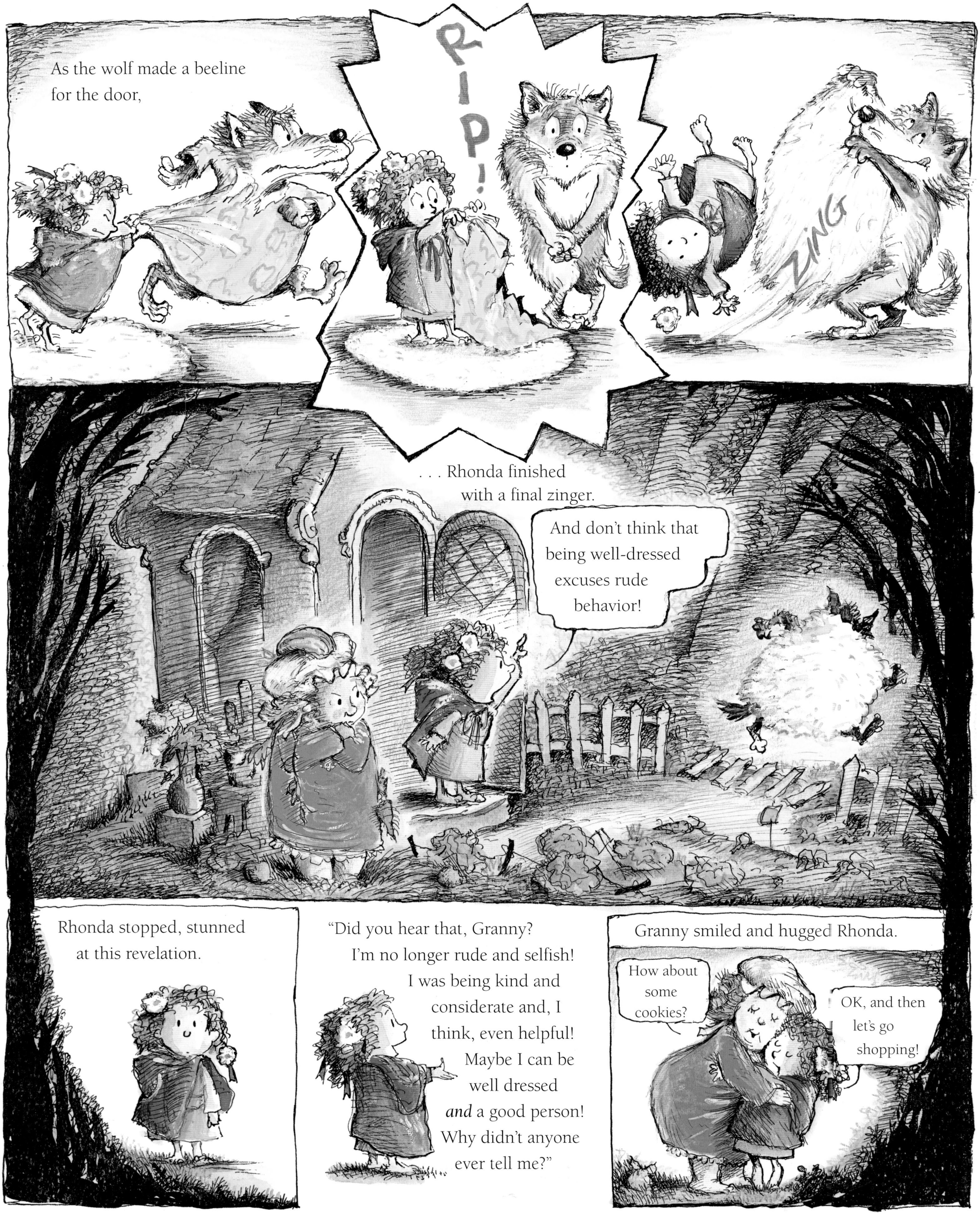
As the wolf made a beeline for the door,
RIP!
ZING
. . . Rhonda finished with a final zinger.
And don't think that being well-dressed excuses rude behavior!
Rhonda stopped, stunned at this revelation.
"Did you hear that, Granny? I'm no longer rude and selfish! I was being kind and considerate and, I think, even helpful! Maybe I can be well dressed *and* a good person! Why didn't anyone ever tell me?"
Granny smiled and hugged Rhonda.
How about some cookies?
OK, and then let's go shopping!

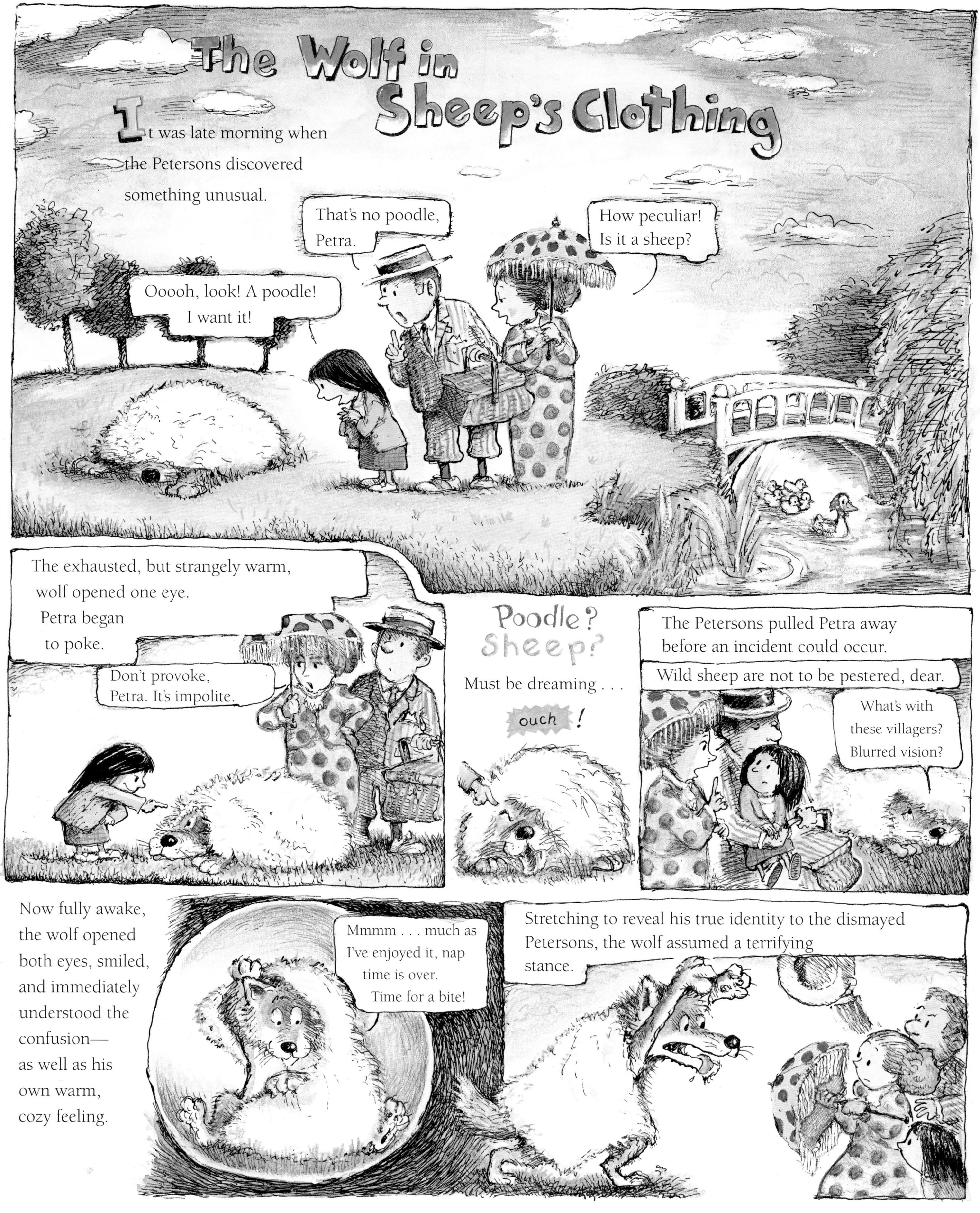

The Wolf in Sheep's Clothing
It was late morning when the Petersons discovered something unusual.
Ooooh, look! A poodle! I want it!
That's no poodle, Petra.
How peculiar! Is it a sheep?
The exhausted, but strangely warm, wolf opened one eye. Petra began to poke.
Don't provoke, Petra. It's impolite.
Poodle? Sheep?
Must be dreaming . . .
ouch!
The Petersons pulled Petra away before an incident could occur.
Wild sheep are not to be pestered, dear.
What's with these villagers? Blurred vision?
Now fully awake, the wolf opened both eyes, smiled, and immediately understood the confusion— as well as his own warm, cozy feeling.
Mmmm . . . much as I've enjoyed it, nap time is over. Time for a bite!
Stretching to reveal his true identity to the dismayed Petersons, the wolf assumed a terrifying stance.

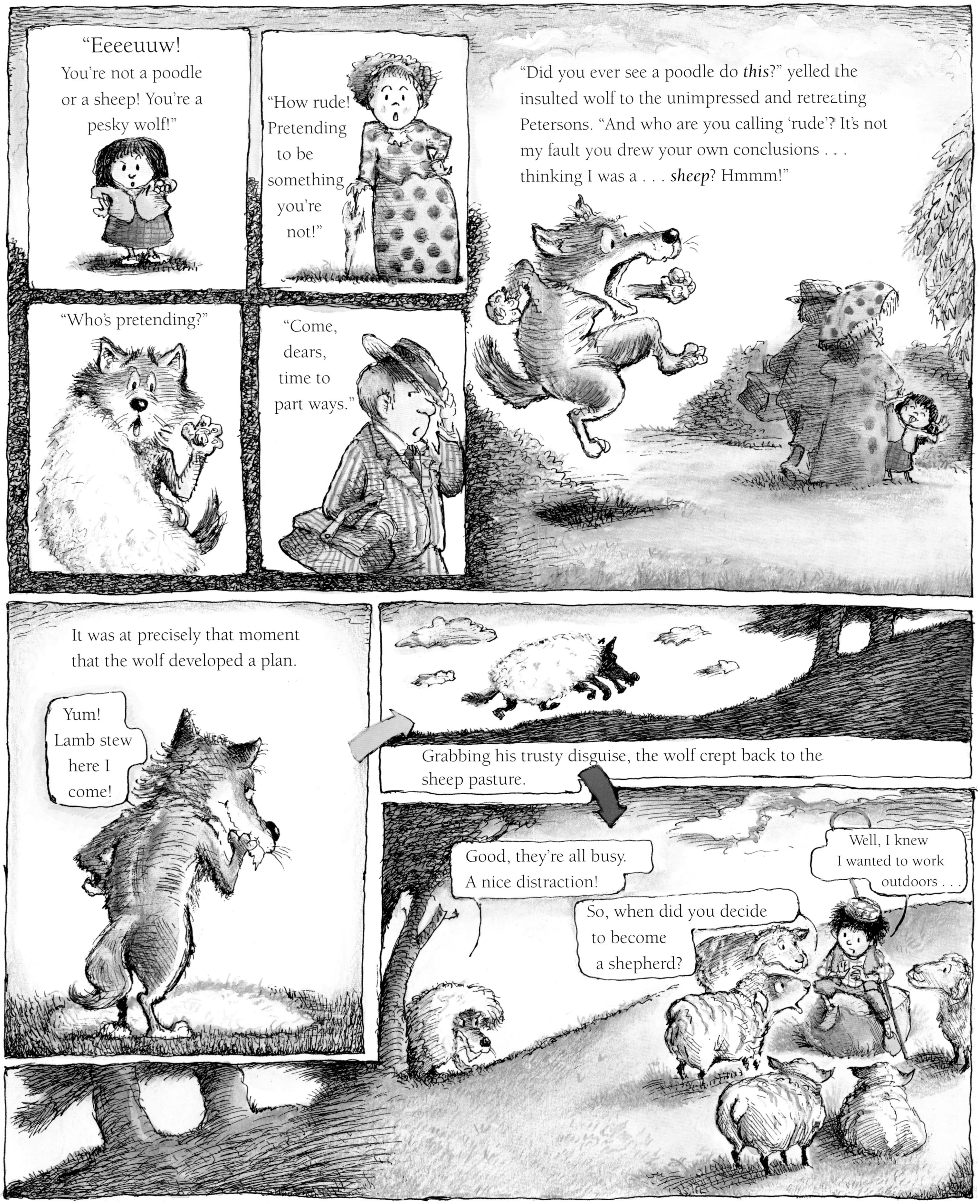
"Eeeeuuw! You're not a poodle or a sheep! You're a pesky wolf!"
"How rude! Pretending to be something you're not!"
"Who's pretending?"
"Come, dears, time to part ways."
"Did you ever see a poodle do *this*?" yelled the insulted wolf to the unimpressed and retreating Petersons. "And who are you calling 'rude'? It's not my fault you drew your own conclusions . . . thinking I was a . . . *sheep*? Hmmm!"
It was at precisely that moment that the wolf developed a plan.
Yum! Lamb stew here I come!
Grabbing his trusty disguise, the wolf crept back to the sheep pasture.
Good, they're all busy. A nice distraction!
So, when did you decide to become a shepherd?
Well, I knew I wanted to work outdoors . . .

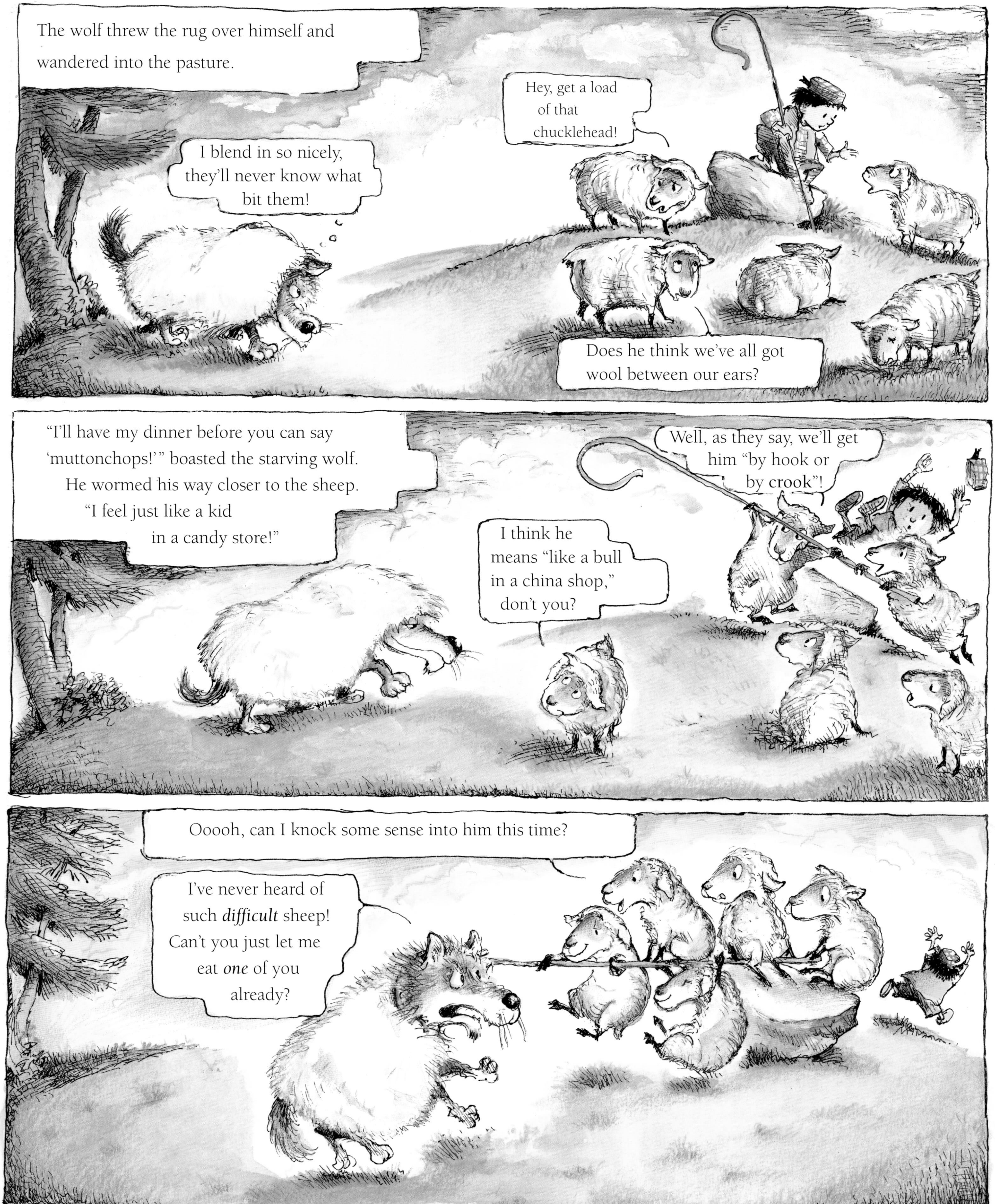
The wolf threw the rug over himself and wandered into the pasture.
I blend in so nicely, they'll never know what bit them!
Hey, get a load of that chucklehead!
Does he think we've all got wool between our ears?
"I'll have my dinner before you can say 'muttonchops!'" boasted the starving wolf. He wormed his way closer to the sheep. "I feel just like a kid in a candy store!"
I think he means "like a bull in a china shop," don't you?
Well, as they say, we'll get him "by hook or by crook"!
Ooooh, can I knock some sense into him this time?
I've never heard of such *difficult* sheep! Can't you just let me eat *one* of you already?

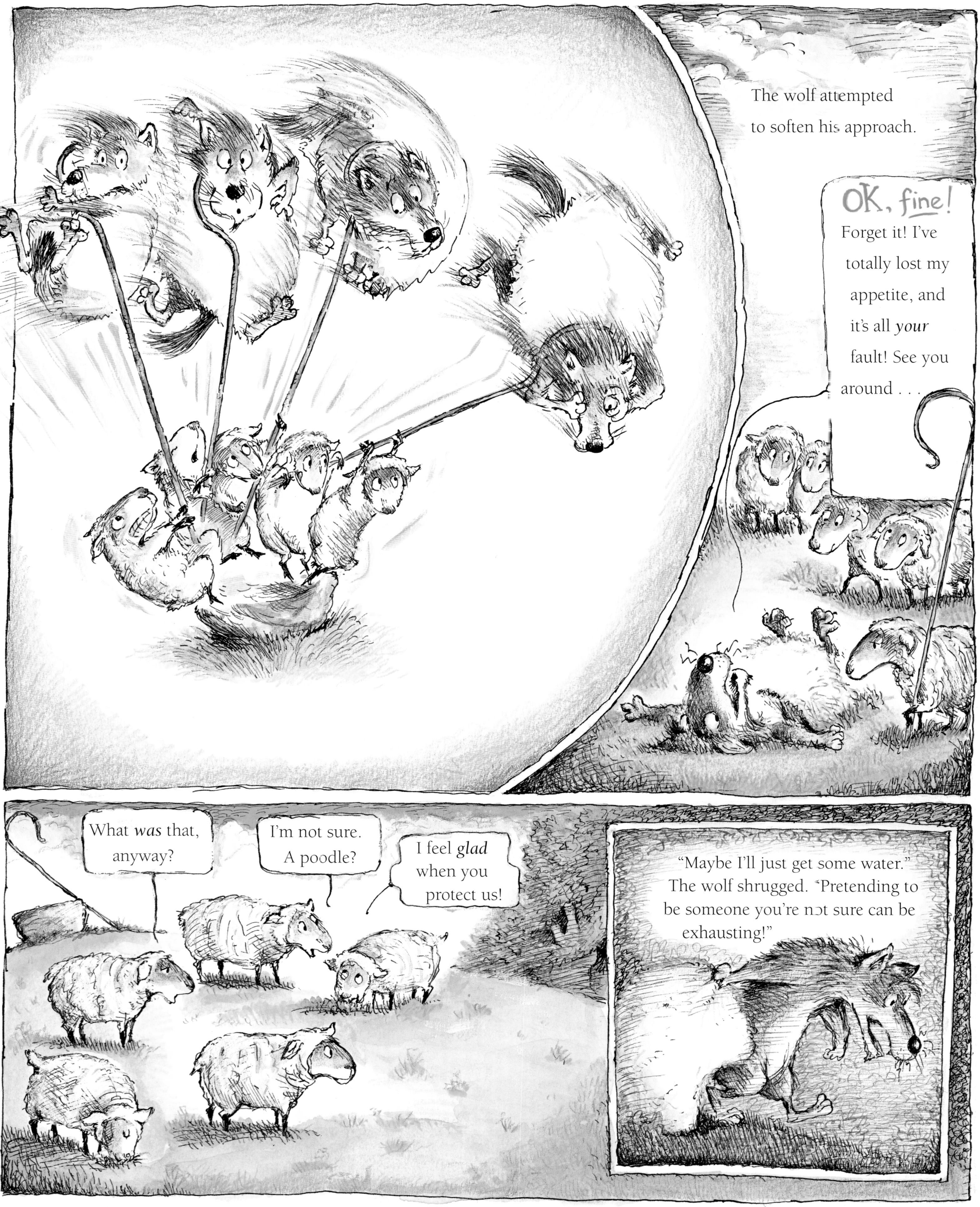
The wolf attempted to soften his approach.
OK, *fine!*
Forget it! I've totally lost my appetite, and it's all *your* fault! See you around . . .
What *was* that, anyway?
I'm not sure. A poodle?
I feel **glad** when you protect us!
"Maybe I'll just get some water." The wolf shrugged. "Pretending to be someone you're not sure can be exhausting!"

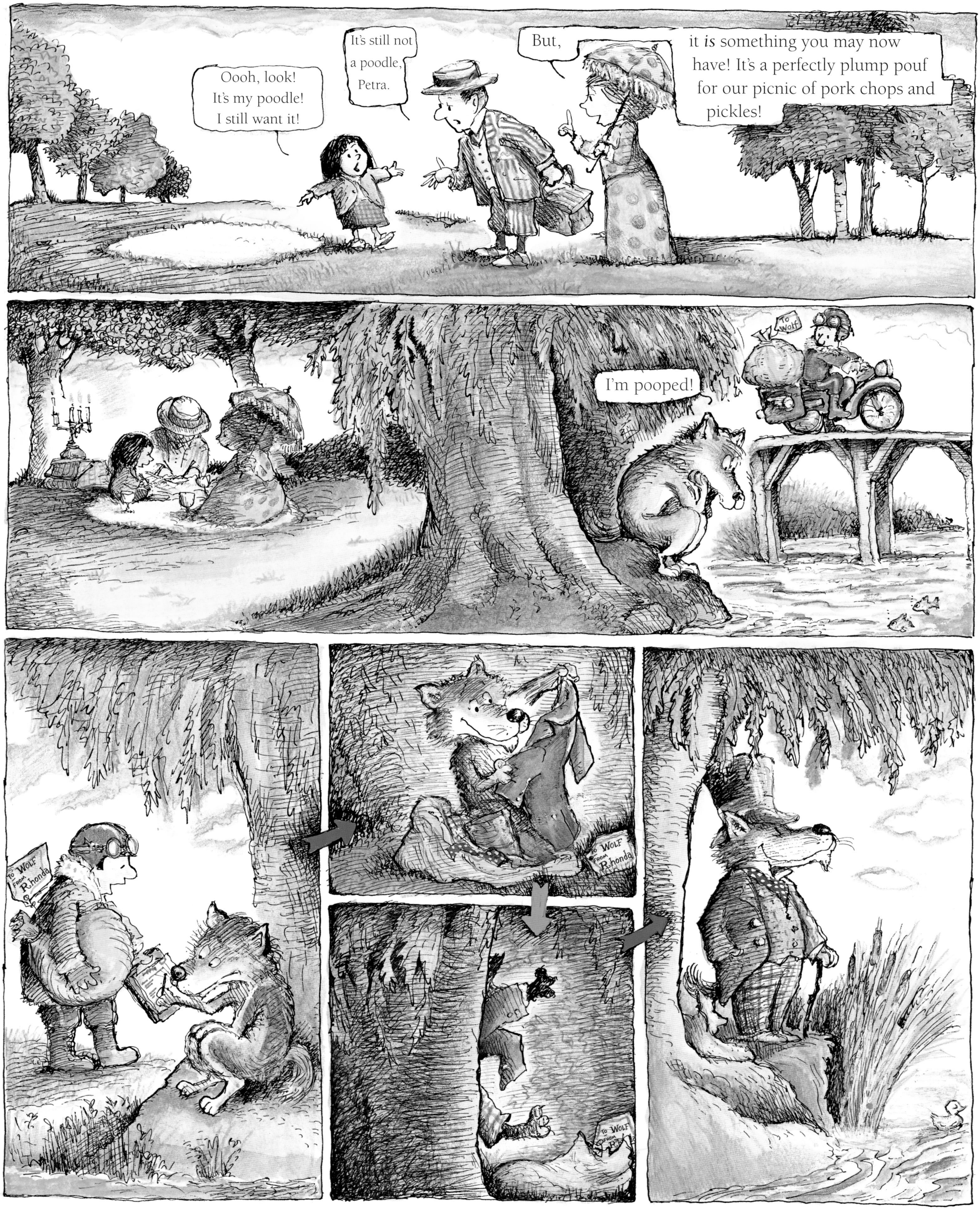
Oooh, look! It's my poodle! I still want it!
It's still not a poodle, Petra.
But, it *is* something you may now have! It's a perfectly plump pouf for our picnic of pork chops and pickles!
TO WOLF
I'm pooped!
TO WOLF FROM Rhonda
TO WOLF FROM Rhonda
TO WOLF FROM

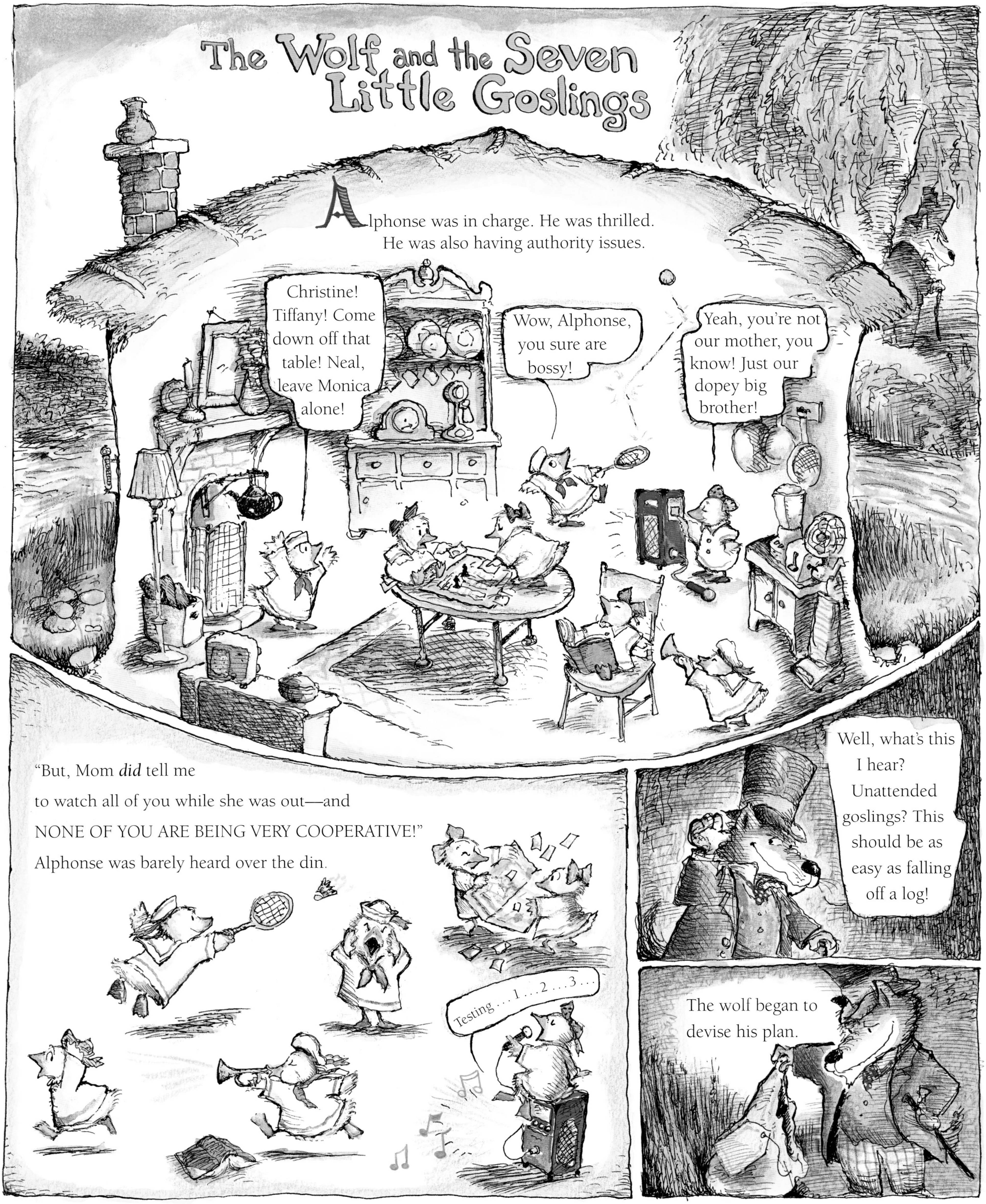
The Wolf and the Seven Little Goslings
Alphonse was in charge. He was thrilled. He was also having authority issues.
Christine! Tiffany! Come down off that table! Neal, leave Monica alone!
Wow, Alphonse, you sure are bossy!
Yeah, you're not our mother, you know! Just our dopey big brother!
"But, Mom *did* tell me to watch all of you while she was out—and NONE OF YOU ARE BEING VERY COOPERATIVE!" Alphonse was barely heard over the din.
Testing . . . 1 . . . 2 . . . 3 . . .
Well, what's this I hear? Unattended goslings? This should be as easy as falling off a log!
The wolf began to devise his plan.

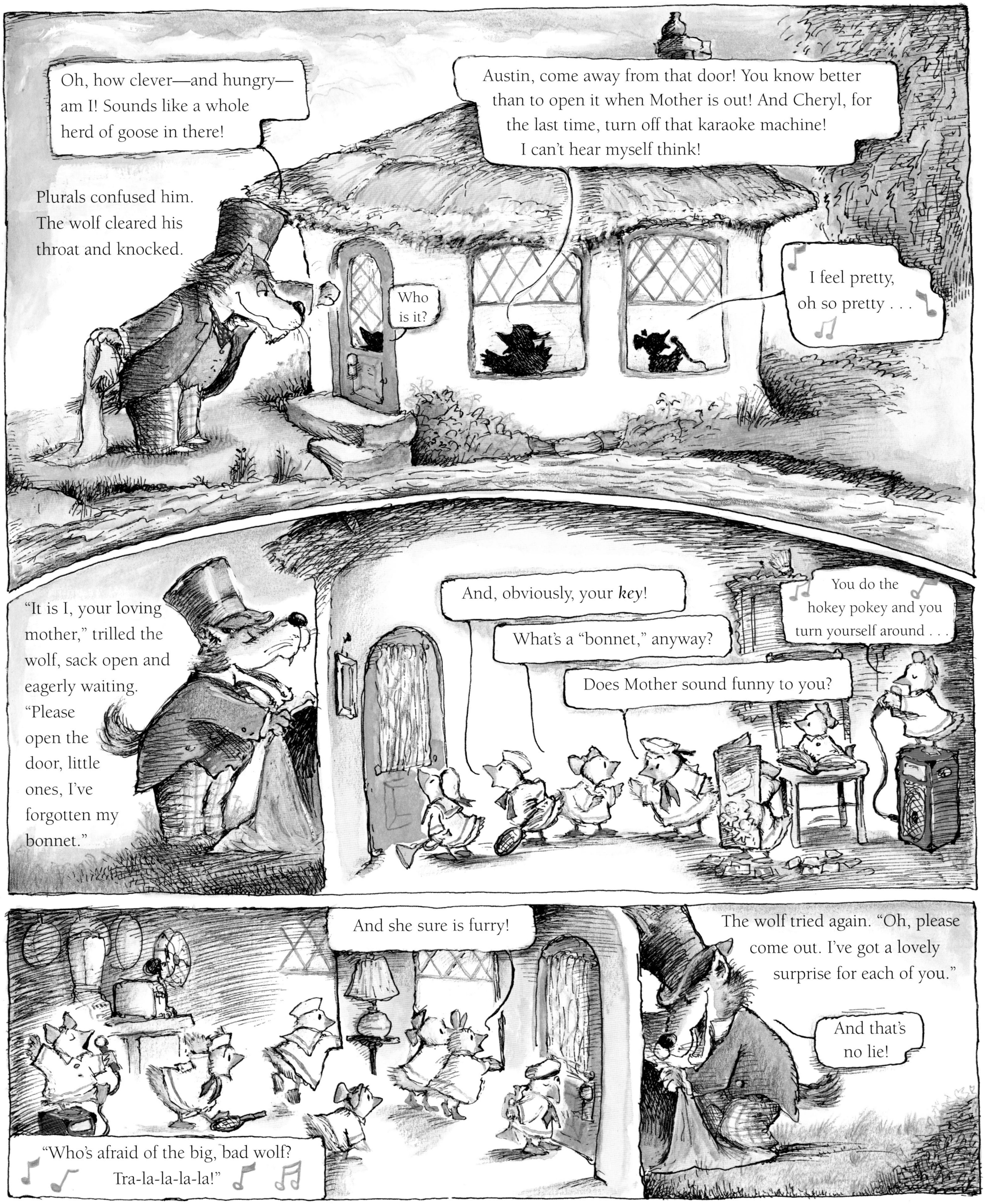
Oh, how clever—and hungry—am I! Sounds like a whole herd of goose in there!
Plurals confused him. The wolf cleared his throat and knocked.
Who is it?
Austin, come away from that door! You know better than to open it when Mother is out! And Cheryl, for the last time, turn off that karaoke machine! I can't hear myself think!
I feel pretty, oh so pretty . . .
"It is I, your loving mother," trilled the wolf, sack open and eagerly waiting. "Please open the door, little ones, I've forgotten my bonnet."
And, obviously, your *key*!
What's a "bonnet," anyway?
Does Mother sound funny to you?
You do the hokey pokey and you turn yourself around . . .
"Who's afraid of the big, bad wolf? Tra-la-la-la-la!"
And she sure is furry!
The wolf tried again. "Oh, please come out. I've got a lovely surprise for each of you."
And that's no lie!

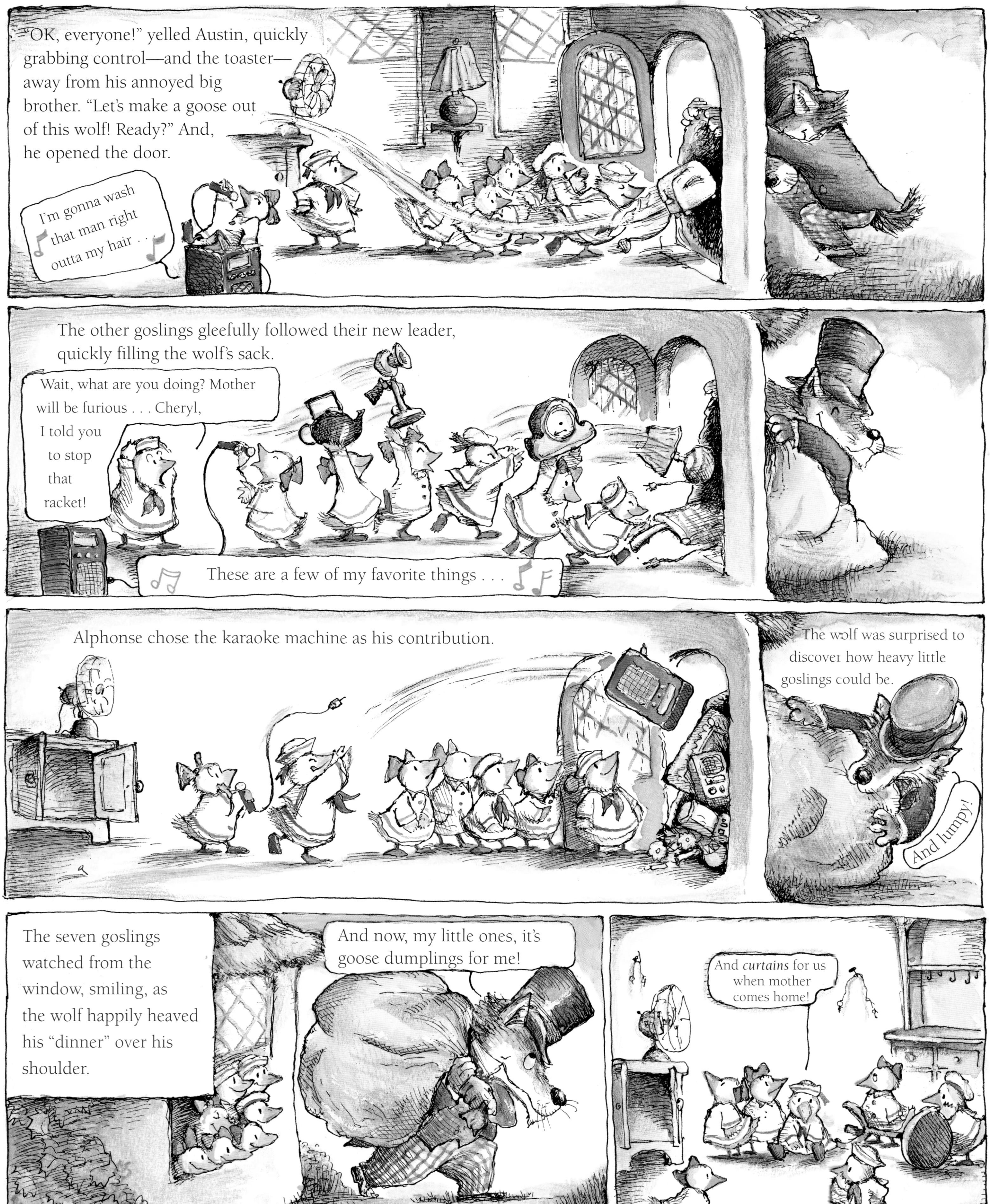
"OK, everyone!" yelled Austin, quickly grabbing control—and the toaster—away from his annoyed big brother. "Let's make a goose out of this wolf! Ready?" And, he opened the door.
I'm gonna wash that man right outta my hair . . .
The other goslings gleefully followed their new leader, quickly filling the wolf's sack.
Wait, what are you doing? Mother will be furious . . . Cheryl, I told you to stop that racket!
These are a few of my favorite things . . .
Alphonse chose the karaoke machine as his contribution.
The wolf was surprised to discover how heavy little goslings could be.
And lumpy!
The seven goslings watched from the window, smiling, as the wolf happily heaved his "dinner" over his shoulder.
And now, my little ones, it's goose dumplings for me!
And *curtains* for us when mother comes home!

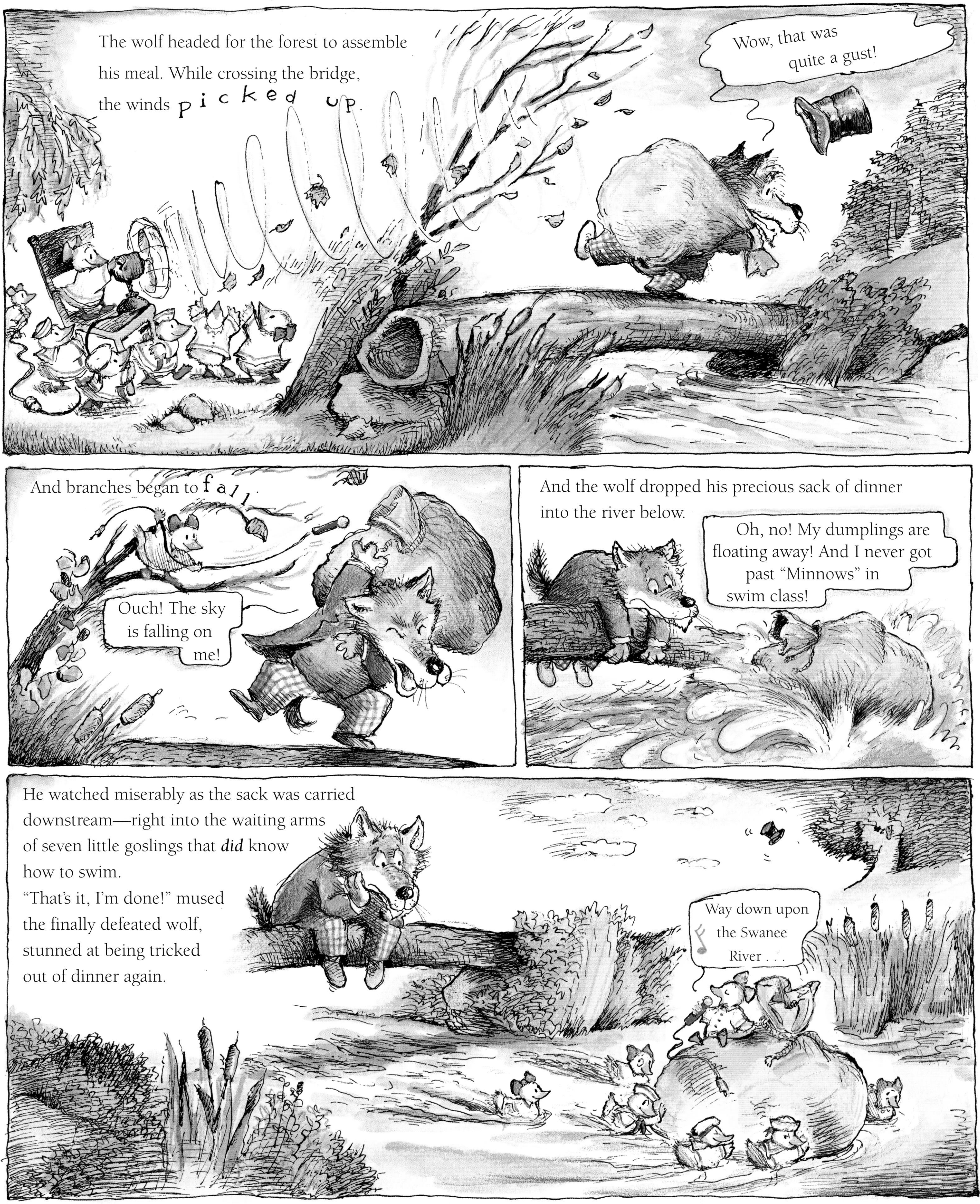
The wolf headed for the forest to assemble his meal. While crossing the bridge, the winds picked up.
Wow, that was quite a gust!
And branches began to fall.
Ouch! The sky is falling on me!
And the wolf dropped his precious sack of dinner into the river below.
Oh, no! My dumplings are floating away! And I never got past "Minnows" in swim class!
He watched miserably as the sack was carried downstream—right into the waiting arms of seven little goslings that *did* know how to swim.
"That's it, I'm done!" mused the finally defeated wolf, stunned at being tricked out of dinner again.
Way down upon the Swanee River . . .

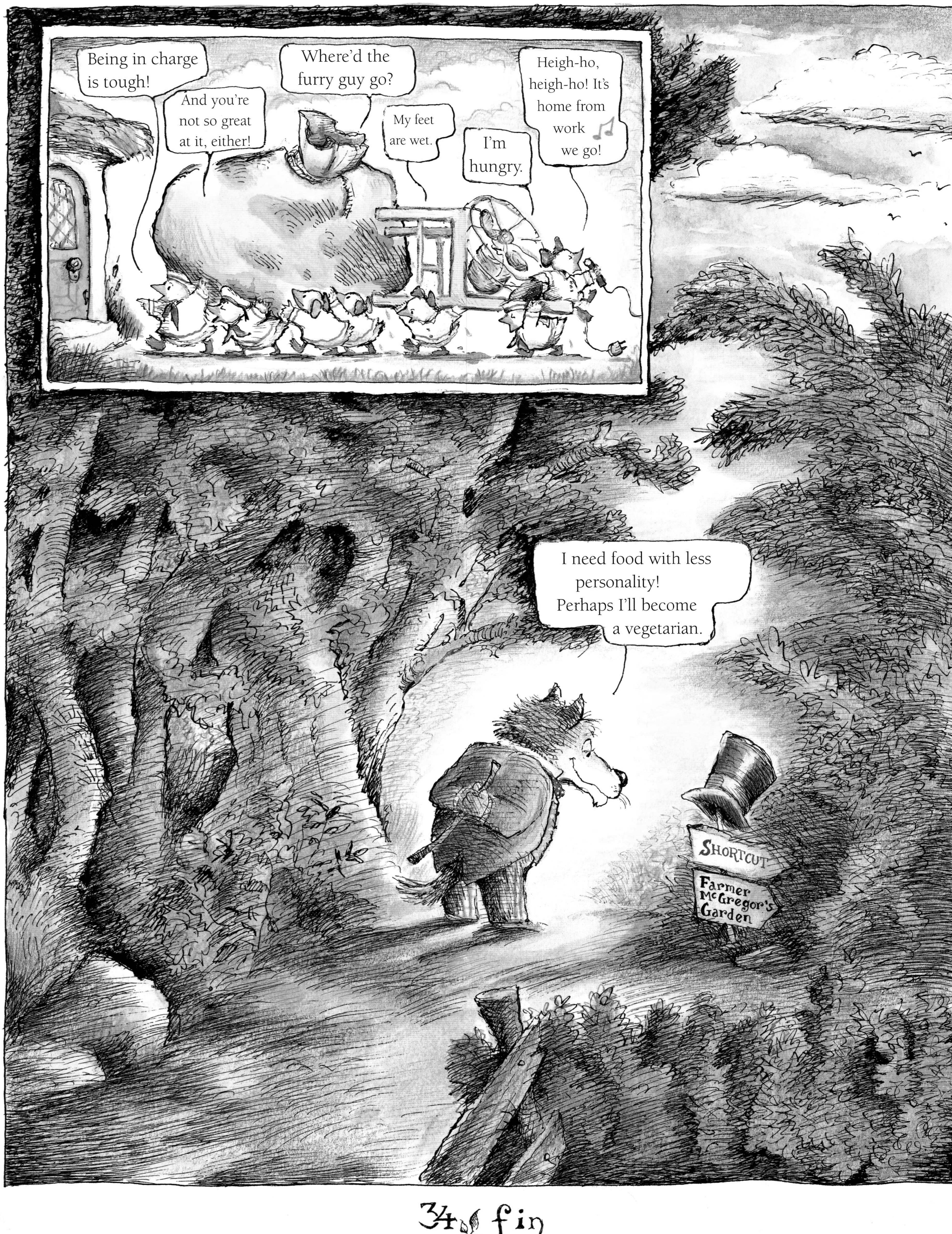
Being in charge is tough!
And you're not so great at it, either!
Where'd the furry guy go?
My feet are wet.
I'm hungry.
Heigh-ho, heigh-ho! It's home from work we go!
I need food with less personality! Perhaps I'll become a vegetarian.
SHORTCUT
Farmer McGregor's Garden

 fin